Dear Romance Reader,

Welcome to a world of breathtaking passion and never-ending romance.

Welcome to *Precious Gem Romances*.

It is our pleasure to present *Precious Gem Romances*, a wonderful new line of romance books by some of America's best-loved authors. Let these thrilling historical and contemporary romances sweep you away to far-off times and places in stories that will dazzle your senses and melt your heart.

Sparkling with joy, laughter, and love, each *Precious Gem Romance* glows with all the passion and excitement you expect from the very best in romance. Offered at a great affordable price, these books are an irresistible value—and an essential addition to your romance collection. Tender love stories you will want to read again and again, *Precious Gem Romances* are books you will treasure forever.

Look for eight fabulous new *Precious Gem Romances* each month—available only at Wal★Mart.

Lynn Brown, Publisher

TEXAS LADY

Donna Delaney

Zebra Books
Kensington Publishing Corp.
http://www.zebrabooks.com

ZEBRA BOOKS are published by

Kensington Publishing Corp.
850 Third Avenue
New York, NY 10022

First Printing: August, 1998
10 9 8 7 6 5 4 3 2 1

Printed in the United States of America

Chapter One

Ignoring the blare of horns and the squeal of tires behind him, Mitchell Sullivan swerved to the side of the freeway and stared in disbelief. Strategically located on the busiest freeway for all of Houston to see was a giant billboard plastered with *his* picture and big bold lettering.

WANTED:
SWEET TEXAS LADY
Send Picture and Résumé to
MITCH
P.O. Box 222
Houston, TX 77928

Traffic came to a grinding halt, but Mitch didn't notice. All he could see was a huge rendition of his own face smiling back at him. All he could feel was a simmering rage.

The continuous blare of horns finally brought him out of his stupor. He shifted gears in his white Mazda sports car and sped off, weaving his way through the infamous Houston traffic with one thought in mind: he was going to throttle whoever did this. He already had a pretty good idea who was behind the prank.

"Curtis, you're a dead man," he murmured between clenched teeth. *Curtis.* The ultimate joker and sometimes, unfortunately, his best friend.

Driving more recklessly than necessary, Mitch whipped his car onto the Fannin Street exit. While he sat at the stoplight, he fumed and thought of different methods of revenge. Chinese water torture, perhaps. Hell, that was too easy. Maybe he could—

Suddenly a car that made his windows rattle with the booming bass of loud music pulled up next to him. Mitch glanced over in annoyance, snagging the attention of the woman in the passenger seat. Her mouth popped open, and she motioned to the other two women in the car. The windows rolled down and the horn beeped and blared. The women waved, blew kisses and hung out of the car windows, whistling and encouraging him to pull over. And much to Mitch's horror, one woman flashed him more of her chest than he cared to see.

"Hey, billboard man, I'm willing, ready and available, baby!" she called over the blaring music.

Damn! They had spotted it.

Mitch gave them a weak smile and groaned. Oh, Lord, it had already started. All he needed in his life right now were more women who teased and flirted with him, vying for his attention. As a freelance photographer, it was part of his job to cajole and flirt in order to get the most from his models. But in his personal life, he was entirely different. He didn't care for bold, flirtatious women. He'd been down that hellish road before, and it had cost him. He wanted someone who was soft, caring. A lady.

WANTED . . . SWEET TEXAS LADY.

But dammit, he preferred to find his own women! Now, thanks to Curtis, the choice had been taken out of his hands. Mitch knew it had been awhile since he'd seriously dated, but he was in no hurry to tie himself to a clinging female. It was clear, though, that Curtis had other ideas. Or maybe Mitch was just the brunt of another of his mischievous pranks. Whatever it was, this time Curtis had gone too far.

Mitch averted his gaze and attempted to ignore the women next to him. They hadn't stopped their wolf whistles. If anything, the whistles had become louder and more persistent.

Thankfully, and not a moment too soon as far as he was concerned, the light changed to green and Mitch zoomed off, driving around the block several times and darting through numerous parking lots in order to lose the car full of women with raging hormones. Finally, they gave up their pursuit and he pulled into a parking place at Brady's, the usual hangout where he had arranged to meet the guys. He could hardly wait to get inside and put his hands around Curtis's neck. The man might be almost twice his size, but right now, Mitch was livid. Adrenaline was on his side; Curtis didn't stand a snowball's chance in hell.

The usual boisterous Friday night haze of voices greeted him as he walked through the door to the Irish pub. Brady's was decorated in kelly green, the walls the same shade as the curtains. The dark oak floors and matching tables gleamed from years of polish. An ornate antique bar supported by brass columns stood in the center of the room.

It didn't take long to find his group. As always, they were in their favorite corner booth, and they were the loudest.

"Hey, Mitch! Over here," Skip called across the room, and waved. "Everybody, look! It's Houston's most available bachelor."

Mitch groaned, his face burning as practically the entire room turned to survey him.

"Never thought the ultimate macho man himself would have to resort to such desperate means to find a lady," Skip added, rather loudly. Too loudly, for it seemed as if the hum of conversation throughout the bar had ceased.

"Yeah, Mitch. If I had known you needed a woman that bad, I could have fixed you up with someone, buddy," another so-called friend chimed in.

Stay calm, Sullivan, he told himself as he strolled over to the table. But that was damned difficult to do with every eye in the place trained on him.

He reached the booth where his friends had gathered, each with a snoot full of beer under his belt and sporting a Cheshire smile like an idiot.

"Hey there, guys," he said, forcing a smile despite his fury. "Where's Curtis?"

Straight black hair pulled back into a ponytail and dark eyes dancing with mischief, Skip piped up, "Curtis called and said he couldn't make it."

"Couldn't make it? Don't tell me he's got a date," Mitch scoffed, crossing his arms over his chest.

Skip snickered as he took another swig of beer. "No, no, it's not a date, officially, but he said his evening will be busy interviewing babes."

"Interviewing babes?" Mitch repeated, not at all sure he had heard right. Surely it was too soon to have received any responses from the billboard. Then again, knowing Curtis it was hard to tell how many billboards had been rented and how long his face had been gracing the freeways of Houston.

"Yeah," Skip answered, then added in a loud voice, "for Houston's most eligible bachelor!"

Mitch winced. The rest of the guys at the table chuckled. His hand itched to punch each and every one of them, but he knew it wouldn't do any good. They were too tanked to feel anything anyway. Apparently, they'd all known about the prank, but the ring leader had to have been Curtis. He was the only one who had the balls to do something like this.

Still smiling, Mitch leaned over, placed both hands on the table and said in a deadly calm voice, "You tell Curtis, I'll find him. And when I do, I'm going to rearrange that ugly face of his."

The chuckling ceased, and every one of them swallowed hard at the menacing look Mitch gave them.

"Now, if you'll excuse me, guys, I don't feel much like partying tonight." He started to walk away, but then turned around. "If I find out any of you had anything to do with that billboard, then you'll have to deal with me. And you all know I'm not renowned for my sweet temper." He smiled wickedly and gave them a salute. "Remember that."

"What's the holdup?" a voice asked from the back seat.

Giselle Grant strained her neck to look above the rush-hour traffic. "It looks like some fool swerved across all four lanes."

"Holy smokes!" Janie squealed in her babylike voice and pointed.

Alarmed, Giselle slammed on the brakes. "What?"

"Look at that billboard."

Giselle followed her pointing finger and stared at the handsome face smiling down at her.

"Oh, geez, what a hunk," Anita crooned from the

back seat. She leaned forward and adjusted her owlish glasses to get a better look.

"Yeah, he's drop-dead gorgeous, all right," Giselle admitted, then added, "But what kind of man would advertise himself like that? Something's got to be wrong with the guy. He probably still lives with his mother, wets the bed or, worse, he's trying to prove to himself that he actually likes women. Otherwise, a man who looks like *that* shouldn't have any problem getting a date."

Janie sighed and shook her head, the red curls draped in ringlets around her head bobbing like a Slinky. "You're so cynical, G.G. Just look at him. He's perfect with that thick blond hair, those dark blue eyes. And oh look, he's even got dimples! I just love dimples." She gushed on in Marilyn Monroe style.

"I'll bet he's got a great set of buns," Anita joined in. She shoved her hands to the front and squeezed them into fists.

"Oh, please," Giselle groaned as she inched the car forward. "I swear, you two are always in heat."

"Yeah, ain't it great?" Anita wagged her eyebrows. *"You* could use some heat in your life, G.G. You need a man," she insisted. Rolling down the window of Giselle's black Lexus, she stared at the billboard as they crept along in the traffic.

"Hey, Giselle! Why don't you write him?" Janie suggested, her blue eyes wide and inquisitive. "Hurry, Anita, take down his address."

Anita scrounged around in her overstuffed purse. "Wait a minute . . .

"Got it!" she triumphantly announced a split-second later.

"I don't want his address. If you're so crazy about him, maybe you should write him." A break opened in the traffic, and Giselle sped up.

Anita snorted. "You're the one in need of a man. You're not getting any younger, you know. In fact, I'd be willing to bet your hormones are about to shrivel up and die from the lack of visitation from Big Jim and the Twins."

"Says who? My hormones and I are doing just fine, thank you. Good heavens, Anita, I'm only twenty-six. Not exactly out to pasture, mind you. I've got my own apartment, a wonderful job—"

"Thanks to your daddy," Anita smugly interrupted. "What about love, G.G.? Don't you ever get lonely at night? Don't you ever long to have that special someone in your life?"

"Of course I do! But I'm not going to find him on a blasted billboard!"

Janie added her airheaded two cents. "You never know. He could be the man of your dreams, your Prince Charming, your very own James Bond."

"That man is made of cardboard and glue. For all we know, he could be a serial killer, advertising for his next victim."

"Oh, no. He's not," Anita protested.

"How do you know?" Giselle shot a look at her friend in the rear-view mirror.

"Uh . . . er . . . well, I just know, that's all. He couldn't be some sicko. He's too gorgeous."

Janie laid a hand on Giselle's arm and said in a sincere tone, "James Bond is not made of glue, G.G. And he has a license to kill, so it's legal. Like Anita said, he's not some sick serial killer. Otherwise Miss Moneypenny wouldn't love him after all those years."

For a split second, Giselle tried to follow Janie's train of thought, then gave up. She loved her friend dearly, but would never understand how her mind worked.

"Nita, a normal guy doesn't have to paste his picture on a billboard, for God's sake." Giselle pulled off the freeway. "Let's stop by Brady's for a drink. Okay?"

"Changing the subject, my friend?" Anita asked with a smirk.

Giselle slid the car into park, then commented, "Most definitely."

The women walked to the pub and were about to open the door when a man flung it wide and stormed out. Giselle reeled backward.

"Excuse me," he mumbled as he reached out strong hands to steady her.

"Watch where you're going, buddy." Anita frowned. "I tell you, men these days—" She stopped cold and stared up at the man holding Giselle. "Uh-oh." Her mouth dropped open.

"It's him," Janie whispered.

After Giselle regained her balance, she gazed up at the man whose long, lean fingers still held her. Staring down at her with eyes the color of the deepest blue sea was the man on the billboard. And he was anything but cardboard and glue. He was tall, virile and masculine. Definitely all male.

And available, her hormones screamed.

More like desperate, her mind countered.

"You're really him," Janie voiced in wonder as she sashayed up to him and looked him over as if he were a delectable piece of chocolate cake on a PMS day.

A dark cloud of anger crossed his face, and Giselle was sure lightning would zing out of his eyes at any moment, striking her dead on the spot. But not one bolt of lightning, not even a rumble of thunder followed. Just an abrupt release that left her grasping at the air.

Without another word, he walked away, his back ramrod straight, his muscles tight and bulging as if he fought for control over the anger that radiated from him. His steps were hurried, his stride long, as if he couldn't wait to get away from them. *From her.*

One thing was sure: she certainly had a way with men. Maybe her hormones had deserted her. And the result? Still single at twenty-six.

The three women watched him walk to his car, get in and speed off.

Anita sighed and swiveled her hips. "Oh, Lord, I think I'm in love. He's better than I expected."

Janie sighed too. "He *is* a dream man."

"I knew he would have nice buns. I just knew it." Anita scrunched her hands out in front of her again.

Giselle wanted to agree, but couldn't find her voice. She was too shocked by her reaction to this man. Too dismayed that she would never have the chance to see him again—not in a city this size. And too disappointed that he could be so desperate as to advertise for a woman in such a bizarre manner.

The once comatose hormones sent a tingling warmth through her skin where his fingers had burned into her arms. Absently, she rubbed at the sensation, shaking her head and trying to come to her senses. "You two are pitiful."

"Yeah, sure, like he didn't make your nipples sit up and beg." Anita opened the door to the pub. "Come on, I need a drink. First round is on me."

Several drinks later, while they sat around a tiny table in the corner of the crowded pub, Anita blurted above the blare of the music, "I dare you."

Giselle blinked back. "Dare me to do what?"

"I dare you to write to the billboard man."

"Uh-uh, no way, out of the question." Giselle shook her head vehemently, then regretted it as the room spun slightly from the effects of the one margarita she'd indulged in. Three rounds ago while Anita had plunged ahead, downing one drink after another, Giselle had changed from the potent drink to sparkling water.

"Is this Giselle Grant, turning down a dare?" Anita grinned wickedly.

"Well, I . . . I—"

"I do believe this is a first, Janie," Anita commented as she looked over at Janie who still sat straight up in the chair, her eyes closed and a silly grin plastered on her face.

"Well, she's a goner. So much for getting a second opinion." Anita looked back at Giselle. Her voice rose another notch. "I double-dare you. *And* I'll bet you a thousand bucks you can't get him to date you, even if you wrote to him. No," she shook her head sadly, "the expiration date on your hormones has probably come and gone. You're too old for him anyway."

Giselle choked on the sip of water she had just taken. *"What?* Would you keep your voice down? Good grief, Anita. The way you talk about me, you must think I'm going to be mummified any second now."

"Prove me wrong then. Take the dare and the bet. Come on. If you lose, you can always dip into the trust fund dear old Dad gave you." Anita plopped her chin on her hand and stared steadily at her.

Giselle shifted on her chair. Damn Anita and her bets. They had gotten her into more than one predicament. But then, there was no way she could back down from a double-dare or a bet like that. She'd never hear the end of it. Anita would see to that.

Besides, just from the brief encounter with the billboard man, her hormones were standing at attention, demanding to be noticed. Giselle Grant too old? Ha! Never. She'd show Anita. But more than that, she'd reassure herself that she wasn't quite doomed to a life alone, without love, without passion or her reportedly missing, presumed dead hormones!

Giselle lifted her glass. "Okay, friend, I'll take the dare, but let's make the bet more interesting. Let's up it to five thousand."

Anita touched her glass to Giselle's. "I knew you couldn't resist. You never could back down from a dare, even when we were kids. Now here." She dug around in her purse. Keys, candy wrappers and countless tubes of lipstick littered the table until she finally found what she was searching for. "Here's the address."

Thoughtfully, Giselle took the slip of paper and tucked it in her wallet. She only hoped she wasn't making the biggest mistake of her life. Ordinarily, her existence was in perfect order. Blind dates weren't her thing. They were too risky. If she was honest, lately *any date* seemed to be on her endangered list.

Giselle valued her safe, controlled life too much to take many risks. No, a date with the billboard man certainly wasn't like her. Then again, the weak-kneed feeling she'd had when she'd bumped into him wasn't like her either. Controlled, both emotionally and physically—hormones be damned—that's how she usually was. Her father's constant lectures had seen to that.

"Could I buy you ladies a drink?" A gentleman leaned over their table and bestowed his most charming smile on them.

Before Giselle could say a word, Anita interjected, "Beat it, bozo. This lady is going after the billboard man."

* * *

"You have reached the residence of Curtis Rockwell, stud muffin, love god, the greatest matchmaker of all times. I *am* the greatest!" The mocking imitation of Muhammad Ali's voice came over the line.

Mitch resisted the urge to slam down the receiver. The answering machine continued.

"Sorry, ladies, I can't come to the phone right now, I'm all tied up at the moment. Ooooo, I like the sound of that."

Mitch snorted. "In your dreams, Rockhead."

"And if this is my old buddy, my old pal, Mitch, don't worry partner, I've got it all under control. I'll have a posse of sweet Texas ladies rounded up in no time." Curtis had changed to the slow drawl of John Wayne.

"Until then," next came Arnold Schwarzenegger's distinctive accent, " 'Hasta la vista, baby.' "

With growing impatience, Mitch waited for the beep, but had to endure another minute or so of the theme from *Bonanza*. When it finally came, he barked into the phone, "You're a dead man, Rockhead. You might as well quit avoiding me and take it like a man. I'll catch up with you, and when I do, I'm going to rearrange your face. Tomorrow, Curtis. I want those billboards down by tomorrow!"

Mitch slammed down the phone and raked stiff fingers through his hair. Restlessly, he paced his studio loft. Giant windows lined one wall affording him a panoramic view of the twinkling lights that graced the Houston skyline. But he barely noticed. Even in the openness of the room, he felt like a caged animal. Trapped with no way out. Confined to a situation he didn't ask for.

Tonight had been proof enough. He was the laughingstock, not to mention the obsession, of half the women in Houston. He looked down at the torn sleeve on his shirt.

As the night progressed, things had gotten worse. On the way home, he'd stopped at a station for gas. Before he knew what hit him, a woman had thrown her arms around him and insisted she was the sweet Texas lady he'd been looking for. It had taken him several minutes to pry her loose, and in the process, he'd lost part of his shirt.

Now he knew how it felt to be Tom Jones. Poor guy. The celebrity had lost his share of shirts, while gaining an abundance of women's underwear. If women started throwing their underwear at him, by damn he'd leave Houston for good. That is, right after he tortured and killed Curtis.

Unlike the crazy woman at the gas station, the reaction of the woman he'd bumped into while leaving Brady's was a shame. She'd been beautiful, sleek, long-legged, with black hair that hung to her shoulders like spun onyx and dark green eyes that reminded him of the forest at midnight. Her wildflower scent still clung to his clothes, his hands.

But apparently she'd seen his picture on the billboard, too. And in his mind, that ruled her out. For she was too startstruck. He'd already decided any woman who would answer that ad or be interested in him after seeing the billboard had to be off her rocker.

Like his sister. After five failed marriages, Marlena was broke and alone, yet she still looked in the personal ads daily to find another man. In this day and time, the world was a dangerous place. Mitch didn't want any part of a woman who would take such a risk. A *real lady* wouldn't do that.

Another much more disturbing thought skimmed

through his mind, and he groaned as the possible ramifications hit him. He hoped this publicity wouldn't affect the upcoming bid on Monday. The contract with Grant's Department Store was his big chance to make a name for himself in the fashion world. If all went well and his layouts were well received, his career might balloon to include contracts in New York and Paris.

From what he had heard, old man Grant was ultra-conservative. If the CEO of the most successful department store in the South saw the billboard, Mitch could be doomed before he was even given the chance to prove himself. He was sure Grant wouldn't want someone who had solicited himself on a billboard to be associated with a store as refined as Grant's.

What had started out to be a prank could be the ultimate jinx of his life, taking away his pride, his work, his livelihood, even his chance to find a real lady. All thanks to that baboon Mitch called his best friend.

The pounding wouldn't stop. Giselle rolled over and buried her head under the pillow. But no matter how hard she tried to ignore the persistent banging, whoever it was seemed determined to rouse her from a sound sleep. With eyes open just a crack, she got up out of bed, shrugged into an emerald silk robe and stumbled to the door. "Okay, okay. I'm coming," she grumbled, peering through the peephole, then flipping open the lock.

"Good morning," Anita said in a much too cheerful voice as she breezed into the room. "Rise and shine, G.G. We've got work to do."

Giselle held a hand to her forehead. "Anita, how

can you be so happy and *loud* this time of the morning?"

Anita chuckled. "Nursing a hangover, are we?"

"No, I'm not, but you should be."

"Me? Nah, I know how to cure those things real fast. I just had a margarita for breakfast."

"Oh geez!"

"It's called drinking some of the hair of the dog that bit you." She wrinkled her forehead, then added, "Or something like that."

"What in the world are you doing here so early?" Giselle flopped down on the couch.

"As I said, we've got work to do. You know how the mail runs early on Saturdays." Anita walked to the curtains and opened them with one sweep of her hand.

Giselle moaned and covered her eyes to the blinding morning sun. "Whatever are you talking about?"

Anita placed her hands on her rounded hips. "Your résumé for the man of your 'hormonal' dreams, silly."

Memories of last night flooded back to Giselle. "Oh, no. I thought you might have forgotten about that, considering how smashed you were."

Again, Anita laughed. "Are you kidding? Me, forget about that kind of money? Not one, not two, not even a pitcher of margaritas is strong enough to make me forget that. Do I have to remind you, you're the one who upped the bet?"

"Come on, Nita. You're not going to hold me to that dare, are you?"

Walking into the kitchen, Anita opened the cabinets as if she lived there herself. She shrugged her shoulders and began scooping spoonfuls of coffee into a white filter. "Well, I guess we could skip all that and go straight to the bank. You owe me five thousand."

"But I don't have that kind of cash on hand."

She flipped on the coffeemaker. "Maybe not, but your trust fund is full of it. Make that in large bills. They're so much more impressive."

Wide awake now, her fuzzy head achingly clear, Giselle rubbed eyes that felt like sandpaper, licked lips that were so dry it seemed she'd been in the desert for days. "Nita," she pleaded, "I can't dip into my trust fund without my father knowing about it. You know he keeps tabs on every penny. And I could never tell him what it's for. I'd never hear the end of it."

Anita snorted. "It's write up or pay up. Make your choice."

Running a hand through the thick tangle of hair that fell across her forehead, Giselle sighed, "Okay, you win."

"Oh, goody. I can't wait to spend my money." With a devilish grin on her face, she handed Giselle a cup of steaming coffee.

"Forget that. The bet is still on. I'm going to show you that I'm not ready for a cane and a rocking chair just yet." And, she thought to herself, there's no way I can let my father find out about this bet.

Giselle stood and took a sip of coffee. "Geez, Anita," she grimaced. "This brew is so strong it'll grow hair on your chest."

Anita whipped the cup out of her hand. "Then you can't drink it! I mean, a hairy chest wouldn't sound good on your résumé. That's definitely a big turnoff."

Giselle lifted her eyes heavenward. "I'm getting a shower."

"You need to tell him you've got long legs. Men like that."

"Nita . . ." Giselle warned.

"And big boobs. Haven't met a man yet who could resist those!"

"Would you stop?"

Anita gave her an innocent smile. "I'm just trying to help."

Without a backward glance, Giselle walked into the bathroom and slammed the door. "Yeah, sure. *That* kind of *help* I can do without." With an exasperated sigh, she looked at her reflection in the bathroom mirror and shook her head. "Damn the dare, damn the bet. Double-damn those stupid, male-deprived hormones."

Chapter Two

One week later, and against her better judgment, Giselle found herself riding up to the top floor of a fashionable high-rise in an antique, grated elevator to meet the billboard man.

If it weren't for that blasted bet and my curious hormones, I wouldn't be here, she thought with a grimace. But as it was, he had answered her résumé with a message on her answering machine, saying when and where to meet.

Arrogance. This man was full of it. He hadn't bothered to call back and confirm their meeting place. Better yet, he hadn't even asked whether his plans suited her in the first place. The smooth looks of Prince Charming combined with the manners of a stone-age *me-man-you-little-woman* Fred Flintstone. No wonder he had to advertise for a woman.

It was a good thing her schedule at the office was

flexible. Although few, there were some perks that went along with being the boss's daughter.

"What a gentleman. I wouldn't be surprised if he grunts when he answers the door," she muttered as the elevator continued to slowly rise despite many protesting groans and squeaks. Giselle began to doubt it would even make it to the top, which would suit her just fine. Then she could turn right back around and leave. With every floor that passed, her nervousness mounted. And with that, the hiccups began.

"Oh, geez! Not now," she groaned, taking deep rapid breaths, trying to squelch the nervous habit that had plagued her since childhood. But every few seconds, a bubble of air popped out of her mouth. The funny squeaking sound echoed through the— lucky for her—empty elevator.

But as fate would have it, much too soon, for her hiccups hadn't subsided, the elevator finally came to a grinding halt. As the door squeezed back like an accordion, she tentatively stepped out and searched for Suite 7007.

The James Bond signature gold numbers loomed in front of her. Another hiccup popped out. Then another. The only remedy that worked for her was back at the office. She couldn't very well carry a jar of peanut butter with her everywhere she went. But, God, what she wouldn't do for a teaspoon of Skippy. She lifted a hand to her hair, adjusted her bra strap and took a deep calming breath before knocking on the door.

Seconds turned into minutes. No answer. No 007. Just more blasted hiccups. She knocked again. Still, all that greeted her was silence. Frustrated, this time she pounded on the thick oak door.

"Oh, great." *Hiccup.* "He practically *orders* me to come here, and he's not even here himself," she muttered. How utterly, typically, prehistorically male. She searched her purse for a slip of paper. How dare he stand her up. Especially after her hormones had gotten all ready and primed. After so many false alarms, the poor things really would shrivel up and die.

Hiccup.

Her time was worth a lot more than a futile trip across town. By golly, she was going to give him a piece of her mind.

Hiccup.

Bet or no bet.

Hiccup.

Hormones, dead or alive.

After scribbling a few choice words, she bent down to slip the paper under the door. Suddenly, it was flung open. Her eyes focused on a pair of bare feet, traveled up two tanned, sinewy legs covered in blond hair beaded with water. Her sight-seeing tour stopped at the tiny white towel that barely covered his lean muscular hips.

The paper was crumpled in her hand. Her hormones started to sing the *Hallelujah Chorus.* The hiccups lodged in her throat. One thing was sure, she'd just found another cure. And it was much better than Skippy peanut butter.

"Can I help you?" a deep male voice, not even remotely resembling a caveman's grunt, rumbled, the trace of irritation in it obvious.

Giselle's face burned with embarrassment. She forced her eyes up to meet his sardonic gaze. "I, uh—"

"You." The one word came out as an accusation.

She straightened. "Uh, yes . . . Hi, it's me, all right."

He crossed his arms over his powerfully sculpted chest, his hands briefly brushing the sprinkling of gleaming curly blond hair. The very same silky hair that covered his long legs. Still dripping wet, his hair hung about his shoulders in waves as if he had just rubbed the lustrous strands vigorously with a towel. Moisture still clung to his golden skin.

"What are you doing here? Didn't you gawk enough the other night when you *accidentally* bumped into me?" he demanded, his voice cold, distant. He'd gone straight past irritated to just plain unfriendly.

Confusion hit Giselle like a douse of freezing water. What was she doing here? Not only was he caveman arrogant, this guy had a terrible memory. Or maybe that was why he had trouble getting women. He was a male version of a dumb blonde. Gorgeous, but kind of thick between the ears.

Her voice equally chilly, she replied, "I was told to come here."

"By whom?"

Even though the billboard man stood half-naked in front of her, he seemed in no hurry to make himself more presentable. As it was, she had a hard time keeping her eyes off the white towel. She almost wished she could whip it off of him and use it to dry the tiny drops of moisture sliding down his chest. That, or snap it a time or two in his arrogant face.

But she wasn't just curious or angry, she was wary. He'd answered the door half-naked. What did he have in mind? A roll in the bed on the first meeting? Well, if that was what he had planned, then he was wrong. Dead wrong. No amount of money on a bet, no insistent hum of hormones, not even the thought of her father's wrath could entice her to do something that irresponsible.

"I presumed it was you. I had a message on my answering machine to *report* here today." She couldn't stem the sarcasm from seeping out in her tone.

The stormy expression cleared from his face. With keen, assessing eyes, he looked her up and down. "Legs," he murmured, stroking his newly shaven chin.

"I beg your pardon?"

"You've got such long legs. You must be the model Warren told me about."

Model? Giselle almost snorted. She was anything but a model. She had long legs, all right, but her gams looked like they belonged on Big Bird.

His next words interrupted her thoughts. "My apologies for my rudeness. The name is Mitch. Mitch Sullivan. I thought you were another one of those women who've been pestering me about the billboard. I haven't had a moment's peace for the past week."

Giselle swallowed hard.

He went on. "You've seen it, haven't you? It was damn hard to miss. At least by the way you and your friends acted the other night at Brady's, I presumed you'd seen it."

"Yes, um, I've seen it," she managed to mumble. Confusion grew with every word he spoke.

"The ultimate nightmare." He shook his head, then grinned, and she caught a glimpse of those devastating dimples. For a moment, Giselle quit breathing. The likeness on the billboard was startling, but it didn't do him justice. He had the most amazing eyes. They twinkled like the richest, rarest sapphires when he smiled.

"Nightmare? You mean you didn't put up the billboard?" she asked in a weak voice when she was finally able to speak.

A dark shadow passed over his face. "Hell, no! And when I catch Curtis, I'm going to—" He stopped,

his hands clenched into fists at his side. "Never mind
that. Come on in and we'll get down to business."

Business? Panic raced along every nerve ending,
and Giselle's wariness, along with her confusion,
mounted.

"I'll go get some clothes on. Then we'll take some
preliminary shots for the layout. With those legs,
you're perfect for the swimsuit pages. Old man Grant
ought to love you just fine. Beautiful, refined, classy,"
he told her while strolling across the room to disappear through the doorway.

She tried to concentrate on what he was saying,
but couldn't tear her eyes away from his backside,
even straining her neck to get a last glimpse of it
before the doorway blocked her view. Anita was right.
He did have a great set of buns. And that tiny towel
did nothing to hide them either . . .

His words finally sank in.

"*Grant?* As in Grant's Department Store?" Oh,
Lord, despite the dimples, the blue eyes, the tiny
towel and the great buns, this was getting worse by
the minute. Anita was going to have a field day when
she found out what Giselle had gotten herself into.

"Of course. Didn't Warren tell you about it?" he
asked from the other room.

Warren? Who the hell was Warren? Think fast,
Giselle, her mind urged.

"Er, I guess he forgot to mention it," she stumbled.
Lying wasn't usually her style, and she couldn't help
but feel terrible every time one slipped out. But she
didn't quite know how to gracefully back out of this
situation. She still had a bet to win. It was either that
or suffer the consequences of her father finding out
she withdrew five thousand dollars from the trust
fund. And she most certainly didn't want that.

"By the way, what's your name, honey?"

"Uh . . . Giselle Gra—Green. Giselle Green."

He ducked his head around the doorway from what appeared to be his bedroom. "How appropriate."

She wrinkled her forehead. "I don't understand."

"Legs, honey. Legs as long and as graceful as a giselle's." He gave her another heart-tugging grin and disappeared into the room.

Giselle walked farther into the loft and sank onto the soft earth-toned leather couch. Good Lord, what was she going to do? She didn't know the first thing about modeling. And if she did it, heaven forbid, it would be for her own father's stores. Dad would kill her if he saw her face, not to mention her scantily clad body, in this year's catalog. Legs! She'd use them for running if her father got wind of this.

But then, if she backed down, she'd lose the bet. And she was sure Anita would never let her live it down, even though the situation had changed drastically. Mitch apparently didn't want to find a woman, or so he claimed. By the tone of his voice, if he found out she was here about the billboard, he would probably tell her to take a hike. No, correct that. He would most definitely toss her out on her butt.

But who had called her and left the message? If she remembered correctly, Mitch's voice sounded the same as the one on the answering machine. Deep and silky and smooth as liquid silver.

The hiccups threatened to return. Giselle pressed on her diaphragm hoping to stem them before they got into full swing. She got up, wandered to the giant windows, and admired the spectacular view of the city. Although the day was mostly sunny, the ever-present haze of pollution hovered just above the skyline.

As she stared out, the answer popped into her mind. A coward she had never been, and she wasn't about to start today. In a way, Anita was right. Not just about his buns, but about Giselle herself. She wasn't getting any younger. It was time to get her hormones in gear, time to take some risks. At least the risks involved with Mitch were less troublesome than those with an irate father.

Besides that, Mitch's dimpled smile melted her insides to hot, honeyed butter. An image flashed in her mind of Mitch kissing her, holding her until the melted butter raced through her body like a molten lava flow.

She shook her head. Good Lord, where had that thought come from?

From hormones that have lain dormant much too long, that's where.

Yet she hardly knew this man.

What's to know? He's got great buns and devastating dimples, that ought to be enough.

Even though he did, indeed, have a smile that made her heart turn cartwheels, he was much more arrogant than Giselle cared for in a man.

Honey, if you wait for the perfect man, you will become mummified before your time.

"Okay, Legs," he said as he walked back into the room.

Startled out of her internal conversation with herself, Giselle whipped around. Her hungry eyes feasted on him, from his bare feet to his muscular legs and slim hips, covered in tight blue jeans, up to the denim shirt that hung open revealing mounds of tempting, swirling hair.

"Show me what you've got."

Giselle swallowed her shock. "I beg your pardon?"

Mitch pulled back a heavy curtain. Behind it, a corner in the room had been set aside to hold scores of camera equipment, lights, props and backdrops. He turned and raised one eyebrow at her.

"First I want to see your portfolio."

"I, uh, I didn't bring it."

"Did you leave it with Warren?" he asked, his expression growing impatient.

"Yeah, something like that," she mumbled. The hole of deception gaped larger, the lies making it deeper and deeper. Almost too deep for her to claw her way out.

"Then we'll start from scratch. Your clothes, honey. Take off your clothes."

"My clothes?" she managed to squeak. What kind of photographer was this guy anyway? Any minute now the hiccups would start. She could feel them coming on. But for once, she was even too nervous for that bad habit. His presence seemed to keep those irritating pockets of air locked in her throat.

"Is there an echo in this room, or are you hard of hearing?" he sighed with exasperation.

Giselle shifted from one foot to the next.

At her silence, Mitch asked, "Didn't you wear a bathing suit under that? Or bring one with you?"

"Er, no . . ."

Mitch swore under his breath. "Didn't Warren tell you *anything*?"

Quite honestly, Giselle answered, "No, he didn't tell me a thing." If she knew who Warren was, she'd like nothing more than to slap him silly at the moment.

Raking a hand through his still-damp hair, Mitch simply stared at her. His eyes narrowed and Giselle thought for sure he was about to call her bluff.

"Okay, Legs, we'll do it this way." He disappeared into his bedroom and came out seconds later with a white cotton shirt in his hands. He tossed it at her.

"Go change into this. Roll the sleeves up, turn up the collar and leave the first three buttons undone. That ought to do, so I can get a better idea of how well you photograph."

Giselle caught the shirt with trembling hands. Knowing she was definitely in over her head on this one, she debated a moment longer before she turned in the direction of the bedroom.

All this could be solved in an instant if she would tell him the truth. She had to. She should. Once she stepped in front of that camera, he was bound to know she wasn't a model.

For reasons Giselle didn't understand, she ignored all logic, and the urge to hiccup, and slipped out of her dress. She unsnapped her bra and donned the shirt as instructed, leaving nothing on except a wispy piece of underwear. The shirt came to mid-thigh, the unbuttoned V revealed a full cleavage no matter how hard she tried to make it less noticeable.

The wooden floor felt cool beneath her bare feet as she padded back into the main room. "Okay, I'm ready," she said, her voice breathless, her nerves on edge. Any minute, he would know, and she would lose the bet. He might even toss her out just as she was, with nothing on but the shirt. That would look just great plastered on the society pages or, worse yet, the tabloids. Lord, she could see it now—DEPARTMENT STORE HEIRESS CAUGHT PRACTICALLY NAKED!

Mitch glanced up from the camera, back down again, then jerked his head up and stared. His blue eyes darkened, his mouth parted slightly as if he were surprised.

He cleared his throat. "Great. Legs, you look great. I, uh, come over here and straddle this chair and we'll get started."

As Giselle sat down, Mitch turned on the stereo. Sensual, swaying music filled the room. The beats matched the rhythm of Giselle's pulse that accelerated with every passing minute. Any second now, he would find out she was a fraud, that indeed she was here to answer the blasted billboard ad. And any second the hiccups would start and she'd be mortified.

For a few minutes, Mitch adjusted his camera, fiddled with the lighting and turned on a fan. Then he came over to her and threaded his hands through her hair, tousled it and sent it into loose waves about her head. Giselle resisted the urge to turn her head toward his touch like a lazy cat who loves to be stroked.

His long fingers were practiced, firm and cool. Giselle closed her eyes as he continued to arrange her hair, but snapped them open as she felt a satisfied purr begin deep within her. And this time, it wasn't a hiccup. Somehow, she managed to squelch the revealing sound a second before it tumbled out of her mouth.

Mitch's hands stilled, his voice barely above a husky whisper. "There, that's it, honey, wet your lips. Good." Then his hands went to the V in the shirt, spreading the folds apart.

Automatically, Giselle protested and covered his hands with her own. "No! What are you doing? I thought it was my legs you liked."

Sapphire eyes narrowed. "You're new at this, aren't you?"

"More than you know," she muttered under her breath.

"Just relax, honey. I'm not going to molest you—"

Shucks, a naughty voice mocked inside her brain. She stiffened and scrambled for some control over her enthusiastic hormones. What was wrong with her? She was *always* in control.

Too much control. That's why those little suckers were chomping at the bit to be let loose.

"Since you're going to be the swimsuit model, I need to see as much skin as possible."

That sounded like a line if she ever heard one.

"Look, if you're so inexperienced, maybe I'd better call Warren and have him send over someone else," he warned her, his blue gaze turning to a chilly frost.

Panic gripped her again. Lord forbid he call Warren, whoever that was. Then she would be found out for sure.

"No," she said more sharply than necessary, then her voice softened. "I'm sorry, I'm just a bit nervous. Please don't call Warren. Give me a chance. Please?" Giselle looked up into his eyes and felt the outer world dissolve around her. All she could see were those fathomless pools of the deepest blue she had ever seen.

Silence permeated the room. Mitch stared down at her, his gaze lingering on her lips, the deep cleavage of the shirt. His look was so intense that Giselle was afraid to breathe, to move.

"Okay, Legs," he said softly. His hands moved once again to push open the shirt another fraction. "Let's give it one more try. Good. Just like that. Give me a look that says you want me. Seduce me, honey. Seduce the camera."

And that she did. Because it wasn't all that difficult to do, considering who was behind the camera. She couldn't seduce a piece of metal equipment, but she sure as hell could seduce a living, breathing, warm, gorgeous man. The billboard man. *Her billboard man.*

Dear God, she was in big-time trouble, she thought as the camera clicked and clicked. No longer was the

bet an incentive, or even the fear of her father. She
wanted something else for herself. She wanted to find
out what lay behind the arrogance and the cardboard
and glue. She and her hormones just plain wanted
him—period.

Several hours later, Giselle plopped down at her
desk at the home office of Grant's. She shoved her
purse into a mahogany drawer, took out a jar of Skippy
and immediately punched a number into the phone.

"Anita, get up here. Fast. You're not going to
believe it. Never mind. I'll tell you when you get up
here."

Almost before she had time to turn around, Anita
pranced into her spacious office, then stopped in her
tracks. "Good Lord, G.G., what on earth happened
to you?"

Momentarily, Giselle had forgotten her hair had
been thoroughly tousled by cool, delicious hands.
Her scalp still tingled from his touch.

She whipped out a mirror and brush, and straightened her appearance. "You wouldn't believe me if I
told you."

"Wow, you two must have *really* hit it off. Gosh, on
the first date, too," Anita said. Pulling up a chair,
she rested her chin on her hand. "Tell me all about
it. I want to hear every last juicy detail."

"Oh, hush, it's not like that. It's much worse."
Giselle returned the mirror and brush to a drawer in
her desk. Then she dipped a finger into the thick
peanut butter, pulled it out and popped it in her
mouth.

"Hiccups again?"

"Had them all day, off and on. Can't imagine why,
can you?"

"He wants to marry you, doesn't he? The nervous bride already!"

"Not hardly." Giselle groaned and dropped her face in her hands. "He wants to take my picture."

"Your picture? For what? Is this guy some kind of porno king?" Anita asked, and for once her voice sounded more concerned than amused.

"Get this. He's the photographer contracted to produce this year's late summer catalog for none other than Grant's Department Store."

"Oh, boy—"

"And, there's more. He thinks I was sent to his apartment by some guy named Warren as a prospective model."

"Uh-oh."

"Wait, that's not all. He didn't put up that billboard, or so he claims."

Anita frowned. "Then who called you and left the message?"

Giselle shook her head. "I have no idea. The voices match, but when the subject came up about the billboard, he was livid. He mentioned the name Curtis, but other than that, I don't know what's going on."

"Er, uh, you said Curtis?" Anita cleared her throat and shifted in her chair.

Suspicious at her friend's obvious nervousness, Giselle studied Anita with determined eyes. "Yeah. What about him? Are you holding out on me, Nita? Tell me," she demanded. "What do you know about this Curtis guy?"

"Uh . . . nothing. Nothing at all," Anita insisted. "I just thought maybe Mitch tried to blame the billboard on someone else. Maybe he's embarrassed about having to advertise for a woman and the model thing is just a cover."

Giselle got up and paced the pale blue carpeted

floor. "No, I don't think so. He's legit. The guy is none other than Mitch Sullivan. I remember Daddy mentioned Sullivan Studio got the contract for the ad campaign this year."

"Why did he think you were a model?"

Giselle looked down and simply said, "Legs."

Somehow the word didn't sound half as sensual when it came from her lips as when Mitch said it. All afternoon, that's what he had called her. The word had become almost like a caress. And in spite of her present turmoil, the memory brought a tiny smile to her face.

"And you didn't bother to correct him," Anita commented with a smirk.

"He recognized me from the other night at Brady's."

" Oh—"

"And he seemed so hostile about it, that I had to think fast. So I just went along with his presumption." She stopped her pacing and flopped back down on the highback leather chair. "I hate being dishonest, but once the ball got rolling, I just couldn't seem to stop it. At first, I thought about the bet, and how Dad would react to a large withdrawal, but then—"

Anita finished her thought as she often did. "But then the hormones kicked in and it became more personal. Is he as gorgeous as he was on the billboard and in the sneak peek we got at Brady's?"

Giselle moaned and leaned her head against the back of the chair. "Ten times more. Unfortunately, he's just as arrogant. But there's something about him . . ."

"Didn't he connect your name with the store?"

The leather chair squeaked as Giselle squirmed. "No, because I didn't tell it to him."

Anita lifted her glasses above her eyes. "You didn't tell him your name?"

"Oh, I told him, all right." She stuck out her hand to Anita and gave it a firm shake. "How do you do? Meet the new Giselle. Giselle *Green.*"

"Well, at least you're still G.G.," Anita chuckled.

"Damn your stupid bet. You got me into this mess."

Her friend raised a not-so-innocent eyebrow. "You didn't have to take it, you know. I was more than ready to go shopping."

Giselle rubbed her aching temples. "Oh, God, Anita, what am I going to do?"

Chapter Three

The shirt still carried her scent. Once again, Mitch held the garment to his nose and inhaled the fragrance that was uniquely Giselle—so soft and feminine, a combination of flowers and the wind. Along with her smell, he could almost imagine the feel of her dark silky hair as it had glided through his hands, the warmth of her ivory skin against his fingertips.

With a reluctance he didn't understand nor could he define, he put down the shirt and walked into the darkroom set up in one small section of his loft. He turned off the overhead light, and the room glowed a dark, crimson red. Stripping the camera of its negatives, he began to develop the rolls and rolls of film he had taken that day.

Excitement grew with every color glossy he hung up to dry. He had managed to catch her sensuality, her essence, her clean, natural beauty. Even though she didn't have the ease before the camera that most models did, something about her made the photographs come alive.

Maybe it was those dark emerald eyes that stared up at him, held him captive, mesmerizing him. Or it could be the way she held her lips, soft, pouting, invitingly wet. Perhaps it was her legs that seemed to go on for eons, long, slim, perfect, her toes tipped with soft pink nails.

Mitch swished the last picture in the developing solution. As the image came into focus, his breath caught in his throat.

"Exquisite," he murmured.

He had photographed countless beautiful women in his life, and men and dogs and cats, even goldfish and snakes for a pet store catalog, but never had his subject come alive for the camera the way Giselle had. This picture was definitely a personal keeper.

She straddled the chair with those long, luscious legs. Her head was thrown back, and wisps of ebony hair blew in the breeze of the fan. The shirt billowed about her, draped off one shoulder to reveal the curve of one creamy breast. Her face held an expression of utter rapture, yet at the same time, a tender look of vulnerability. And for a moment, Mitch longed to see that look as she lay beneath him, loving him, her beauty wrapped around him, the cocoon of her lean legs holding him tight.

The mental picture started the blood pumping through his veins. A needful ache spiraled downward. And he felt himself grow hard.

Abruptly, he gave himself a mental shake. She was his model, for Christ's sake. And Mitch made it a personal rule to never get involved with his models. He'd been down that road with Celeste, and that relationship had ended in disaster. For the sake of himself and the contract, he must maintain a professional distance. However, even as he thought about the rule, he knew it would be damned hard to follow in this case. Too damned hard.

A loud banging at the door drew him away from his internal dilemma and his external arousal. He swore under his breath at the interruption. Luckily, the process on the pictures was nearly finished. He put out the red light, eased open the door and then shut it behind him.

The pounding continued.

"Okay, hold your horses, I'm coming," he bellowed as he took swift strides toward the door. He flung it open and immediately squelched down the burning need to knock the daylights out of the man in front of him.

There was Curtis, his so-called best friend, standing a good head and shoulders above Mitch, clad in baggy blue jeans, a matching shirt with the tails hanging loose and a baseball cap. He held a Big Gulp from the neighborhood quick-stop in one hand and a bag of greasy popcorn in the other.

"Howdy there, pilgrim," Curtis drawled in his best John Wayne style. He glanced above Mitch's head and into the apartment beyond. "Where is that posse of little ladies I promised you?"

The Duke was probably rolling in his grave about now.

Mitch scowled. "I sent each and every one of them hightailing it out of here, *partner.*"

Curtis frowned down at him. "Now, why would you do that? Didn't you like my taste in women? I thought I sent over some right pretty fillies. Especially that last one."

"The only taste you have to be concerned about is the taste of blood when I split your lip for this last, unbelievable prank." Mitch curled his fists into balls at his sides. "Damn you, Curtis, you've made my life a living hell for the last week."

"Yeah, right. Women flocking all over you, and you think that's hell? Tell your sob story to someone who hasn't been around the block." Curtis snorted. "Well? Aren't you going to let me in?"

Mitch had a good mind to tell him to hit the road. Even after a week, his anger still simmered. But as he looked up at his friend, Curtis bestowed on him his most beguiling, innocent smile. Then his shaggy bearded face changed to a pout.

"Pretty please? I'll let you have some of my popcorn. I got it with extra butter." At Mitch's continued stony silence, he added, "Come on, man. The billboards are down. Gone. Vanished. Kaput."

Against his better judgment, with a sweep of his hand, Mitch invited him in. "Make yourself at home. You usually do. But, Curtis, do me a favor and keep your greasy fingers off my equipment." He left his friend to shut the door and called over his shoulder, "You caught me right when I was finishing up some work."

"Oh, really? Pictures of what this time? More pots and pans, furniture and vacuum cleaners? Or is it lions and tigers and bear—oh, my?" Curtis followed him into the darkroom. He set down his cup and reached for a picture.

Mitch stopped the beefy hand before it reached the glossy. "I told you not to touch anything."

Curtis placed his hands behind his back and taunted, "Yes, Daddy."

"No, this time it's more than babies and bunnies. The bid for that big contract I told you about came through this week. These are some preliminary shots I took today of my first model," Mitch informed him as he took down the hanging pictures and organized them into stacks.

"Today? You said she came over today?" Curtis looked at him closely.

"Yeah, poor thing, I almost scared her to death. At first I thought she was another one of your *fillies.*"

Curtis cleared his throat, then took a swig of his drink. While he crunched a mouthful of ice, he asked, "Can I take a look at her? Don't worry, I won't touch the pictures. Hold them up for me."

When Mitch held up the one he had decided to keep for himself, Curtis's eyes widened and he choked, turning around just in time to spew ice all over the floor.

Mitch pounded on his back. "Hey, are you okay, Rockhead?"

Amidst the coughing, Curtis managed to nod his head. "Yeah." He choked some more, then wiped his eyes. "I guess some ice went down the wrong way. Can I take a look at that picture again?"

For the first time since his friend had arrived, Mitch grinned. "She's breathtaking, isn't she?"

Curtis lifted his bushy eyebrows. "Yeah, I thought so, too. And you say she's a model? How interesting."

"Take a look at those legs, Rockhead. How could she be anything but."

Despite the fistful of popcorn shoved into his mouth, Curtis commented with a gleam in his eye, "She couldn't be anything but. Yep, she's definitely a model, if I've ever seen one. You know, she even looks familiar."

"No." Mitch shook his head. "I don't think so. If I had seen her in any other magazine or catalog, I would've remembered her. That's not a face you could easily forget. And those legs . . ."

"You can say that again." Curtis followed him out

of the darkroom and into the den, where Mitch arranged the pictures on the glass coffee table. "I think she's got a great set of, um, er, of assets. Why don't you try to uncover more of her *ass—ets?*"

"Against the rules, Rockhead."

Curtis grunted. "Since when has that stopped you?"

Mitch stilled for a split second. Since when indeed?

Since the recent disastrous liaison with Celeste who had only wanted to use him to further her modeling career. Besides that, he had found most women wanted the big *C*. Commitment. And since he'd been lied to and used, the *C*-word always made him nervous. Actually more like nauseous.

"Well?" Curtis broke into his thoughts. "I asked what's stopping you? If you want her, go for it."

"Rockhead, I know you may find this hard to understand, being the ultimate womanizer that you are, but I don't want to blow this contract. This may be my big chance. And Grant's is ultraconservative. Getting involved with one of the models is too risky."

"Who says you have to get involved? Why not just have a little fun, for once in your life? Why the hell do you think I put those billboards up? You've been a hermit for the past year. So you got burned by Celeste. Not all women are lying, scheming, money-hungry models," Curtis countered, cramming his mouth with another handful of popcorn.

"Didn't your mother tell you never to talk with your mouth full?"

A loud belch echoed in the room. "You're avoiding the subject."

"Or to say excuse me?"

A wicked gleam sparkled in Curtis's brown eyes.

Mitch stood up. "Oh no. Don't you dare. If you're gonna do *that,* step out on the balcony. Last time you dropped one of your bombs, it took me weeks to get that odor out of the place. If I need an exterminator, I'll call Terminex, thank you very much.''

"Say you'll at least give it a try with the long-legged beauty, or I'll let one fly.''

"Out!'' Mitch barked and pointed to the door.

"Here it comes.'' Curtis gave him a toothy grin.

"Have you've forgotten I'm still mad as hell at you? Remember the taste of blood from a split lip?'' Mitch warned. Even though he knew Curtis wasn't the least bit intimidated, he took a step toward his massive friend.

"Okeydokey. Just calm down. Split lip, huh? What a mental picture. Have you forgotten that you owe me?''

"Still holding that over my head after all these years, Rockhead? Well, your time ran out a long time ago for paybacks.'' Mitch gave him a black look.

Curtis held up his hands. "I'm going, I'm going. I've got to call my cousin, anyway.''

"Your cousin? You mean there's more than one Rockhead?''

"Yeah, my cousin, Anita. I don't think you've ever met her. We're planning a reunion.'' Curtis walked to the door, opened it and then turned around and slipped into an Arnold imitation. "I'll be back.''

As the door closed, Mitch wondered how he'd ever become friends with the big lug. They were opposites, that was for sure. Curtis was as crude as they came. A sports reporter with a foul mouth, not to mention bad manners.

But somehow, in college, the two had clicked. Mitch, the rookie football photographer, and Curtis, the colorful sports writer. Ever since those good old days, Curtis had never let him forget that, if it hadn't been for him, Mitch would never have gotten the job with the college newspaper, and Sullivan Studio wouldn't exist.

In a way, Curtis was right. Mitch did owe him. Although Curtis could be charming and funny at times, a sense of indebtedness was one of the main reasons Mitch put up with his obnoxious friend. However, as the years had passed, it seemed Curtis had enlarged the debt to a lifetime commitment.

Mitch sat down on the couch. His gaze roved over the pictures that were scattered on the glass table. And he wondered how in the world he would ever keep his hands off Giselle Green. Or if he really wanted to? Maybe in his own warped way, Curtis was right. Maybe he should go for it, have a little fun. Or maybe getting involved with her would be the biggest mistake of his life.

Giselle and Anita walked up the sidewalk lined with colorful flowers of every kind, to the Colonial-style home. Massive white columns stood along the front of the house. Giant alabaster rocking chairs lined the front porch, a matching swing hung from the ceiling. Located in the affluent neighborhood of River Oaks, this house had been her home for as long as she could remember.

"You're sure your parents won't mind another guest?" Anita asked once again.

Giselle gave her friend a grin. "Of course they won't. You're part of the family, you know that. If I have to report to these mandatory family dinners, then so should you."

"You make it sound like a chore."

"With my father, sometimes it can be." Giselle used her key and opened the huge beveled-glass door.

"He's an old softy inside, G.G."

"Yeah, with you maybe. But with me, that's a different story. I don't think he'll ever forgive me for being born without a stem on the apple."

"You're exaggerating." Anita eyed her over the rim of her glasses.

"I wish." She closed the door and called, "Mom. Dad. I'm home."

An older and petite version of Giselle swept into the room. "Hello, darling." She reached up and gave her daughter a light kiss on the cheek. "And Anita"— she gave her friend a brief hug—"I'm so glad to see you. It's been too long, dear."

Giselle smiled fondly at her mother. It seemed the older her mother got, the more regal she appeared. Neither the salt and pepper hair, nor the soft lines in her face did anything to dispel her beauty.

"I hope you have room for another hungry mouth, Mom."

Joyce Grant took both of their hands and squeezed. "You know we always have room for Anita. Why, she's like one of our own. Your father will be thrilled."

"You're late," George Grant commented from the dining room door.

"Oh, for heaven's sake, George." Joyce waved him away. "She's not late, and besides, Cook isn't ready to serve just yet."

"Hello, Dad," Giselle greeted in a soft voice as she walked up to the man who had always unnerved her, even as a child. "It's good to see you." She touched her lips to his weathered cheek.

Tall as she was, Giselle had to look up to him. Long hours and strain had taken their toll on her father. He had a head full of snow white hair, his face was deeply lined. As the years had gone by, a familiar scowl had replaced the tender smile that used to touch his face.

"It would have been good to see you at your desk sometime today. Where the hell were you?" he demanded.

From years of watching her mother deal with him, Giselle knew better than to cower, no matter how red his face got. "I, uh, I was doing some marketing research in another area." Whereas that wasn't exactly a lie, it wasn't exactly the truth, either. Geez, this was becoming a habit with her. If she didn't watch it, her nose would start growing, just like Pinocchio's. But if her Dad knew the truth, he'd give her a good chewing out.

His keen, speculative eyes studied her for long moments. Then his face broke into one of his rare grins. "Good, that's my girl. Always thinking about business." He patted her awkwardly on the shoulder. "You see, Joyce? All those countless lectures have finally started to sink in."

"Hi, Mr. G.," Anita broke in.

A genuine smile spread across his face. "Anita, my dear, how nice to see you."

"I hope you don't mind if I crash your family dinner."

"No, dear, not at all. And speaking of which, I've been kept waiting long enough." The scowl returned to his face, and he marched back into the dining room.

Joyce Grant gave them a wink, then muttered out of the side of her mouth, "The king awaits his dinner, girls."

Giselle bit back a smile, and Anita giggled. Arm in arm, they walked to the dining room.

Just before they entered the double doors, Anita pulled her back and whispered, "Marketing research? Couldn't you do any better than that? It was more like *billboard* research, if you ask me."

"Hush!" Giselle pushed her into the room.

The four-course meal took an hour to finish, but Giselle hardly tasted the food. Her thoughts were filled with Mitch and the afternoon they had spent together. She was glad that Anita kept her parents entertained with funny stories and suggestive jokes. They hadn't commented on how quiet and preoccupied Giselle had been all evening, if they'd even noticed. Just as dessert was served, the conversation turned to business.

"Yes, I believe Sullivan Studio will give us the best catalog ever," George Grant commented. He took a bite of the praline cheesecake, then looked at Giselle. "I told you his studio got the contract, didn't I?"

Giselle swallowed hard. The creamy rich cheesecake stuck to the back of her throat. "Yes," she finally managed to croak. "Yes, you told me about it Monday."

With a gleam in her eye, Anita broke a Grant golden rule, leaned forward and propped her elbows on the dinner table. "I've heard so many good things about his work. They say he's the best. I think we're lucky to get him."

Giselle kicked her under the table and gave her a warning look.

But Anita went on. "I've also heard his *models* are the most beautiful, especially in the swimsuit line. You know, Mr. G., I just thought of a great idea."

"What's that, dear?" he asked, his tone indulgent.

"I know marketing isn't my field, but I think it would be fabulous if your bungalow down on Paradise Key was used as the backdrop for the swimsuit shots."

The fork fell out of Giselle's hand and clattered loudly against the fine china plate. In barely disguised horror, she stared at Anita.

Hiccup. Her hand flew to her mouth.

Joyce looked over at her. "What do you say, dear?"

"Excuse me," Giselle mumbled.

Sighing, her mother got up from the table. "I'll go get the peanut butter."

Hiccup. Then another and another.

Her father glared at her until she felt her face burn with embarrassment. Then, finally, he turned his attention back to Anita as she began to speak again.

"I mean, can't you see it in your mind? What better place to photograph Grant's swimwear than on the beautiful island, owned by the man himself, George Grant?"

Giselle slid further down in her chair. Anita really laid it on thick. Grateful to see her mother come back into the room, she took the spoon of peanut butter and swallowed it in one gulp.

George Grant fingered his chin. "Hmmm, maybe."

Her throat still thick with the gooey substance, Giselle choked out, "No! That's definitely out of the question."

Her father gave her a sharp look. "Excuse me?"

"Er, well . . ." She swallowed hard. "Flying the crew down to the Keys would be too expensive. There are plenty of beaches around here where the layout could be done at less cost."

"Harrumph. Beaches loaded with clumps of oil and dead fish. Nothing like Paradise Key with its crystal clear water and sugar white sand. Anita's right. The island would be the perfect place. The publicity we could generate alone about the tie between the location and the store would more than make up for the expense."

"But, Dad—"

"Anita, remind me to give you a raise." Her father's comment drowned out the rest of Giselle's sentence. She looked across the table at her friend. Anita had one of those blasted innocent smiles on her face. Even though Giselle sent a murderous look her way— it would have stripped bark off of a tree—Anita didn't appear to notice or, moreover, to care. She was enjoying every bit of this. More than anyone, Anita knew how Giselle had dug herself into an impossible situation. And now her so-called friend was helping her dig it deeper. If it got any deeper, she'd be sucked right down into the center of hell. Although, it seemed as if she'd landed there already.

For another hour, Giselle had to endure listening to the plan to send Mitch Sullivan and his swimsuit model to the island. But as soon as it was polite, she dragged Anita away before any more outrageous ideas could be planted in her father's head.

Once outside, she climbed into her car and turned to Anita. "How? How could you do this to me? I thought you were supposed to be my best friend."

"What? What did I do?"

"Spare me the innocent crap. You know good and well what you did."

"Well, you may not still consider me your best friend, but your hormones will be singing my praises." Anita nonchalantly checked her lipstick in the mirror. "Don't worry about it. It'll work out just fine."

"Oh yeah, sure. Now thanks to you, somehow I have to find a way to tell Mitch I'm not the model he thinks I am." Giselle wearily ran a hand through her hair. God, she didn't want to do that, because hormones and all, she was genuinely attracted to him. She wanted—no, needed—the time to get to know Mitch before she sprang that revelation on him.

"Oh, no, you won't," Anita insisted. "You're going down to the Keys and model your little butt off."

"Then what? What do I do when my father sees the proofs?" Giselle's hands bit into the steering wheel.

"Fiddle-dee-dee, we'll think about that tomorrow," Anita drawled in her best Southern accent.

"Oh pulease! And Dad wanted you to remind him to give you a *raise?* Well, listen to this, you huz, next time, *remind me* not to get involved in any more of your dares or bets."

She started the car and headed for her apartment. From the very outset, she'd had a feeling she was making the biggest mistake of her life. And now, that feeling slithered back into her mind like the evil serpent as he tempted Eve in the Garden of Eden. Like Eve, she'd accepted the offered fruit. Now, it was too late to turn back. And before long, there would be no place to toss the blasted fruit. Especially after she'd already taken that first delicious bite.

Chapter Four

"Two weeks? You want two weeks off right at the beginning of our summer season?" George Grant bellowed, shooting to his feet. He leaned over and placed large hands on the massive desk in front of him.

Despite his menacing, incredulous expression, Giselle held her ground and raised her chin a notch higher. Sometimes there were perks to being the boss's daughter, then again, more often it made life more difficult, for she had to report directly to the head honcho himself.

"Dad, I haven't had a vacation in over a year—"

"Little lady, I haven't taken a day off in over *ten* years. You're a Grant, remember? This store has been in our family for over sixty years. We have to make sacrifices every now and then for the sake of the company.''

Giselle squelched the urge to give a here-we-go-again roll of her eyes. She was sure she'd heard this same lecture while in the fetal position in her mother's womb. Well, maybe not that long, but certainly since she'd started to work for the store. Somehow, this time she had to persuade him to see her side. She must. Mitch expected her to be at the airport on Saturday to fly down to a remote island in the Florida Keys to shoot the swimsuit section. Little did he know, she knew that island like the back of her hand.

It took every ounce of inner strength she possessed, not to mention desperation, to walk up to her father and place a hand on his rigid arm. ''Dad, now would be the perfect time for a vacation. After the photographer gets back from the Keys, I'll be busy distributing the catalog. After that, it's back to school. Then before you know it, Christmas will be here.'' She gave his arm a persuasive little squeeze. ''Daddy, please. I really need some time off.'' And her hormones needed some time *turned on*.

George Grant's scowl softened. ''I'm sorry, Giselle. I sometimes forget that just because this company is my life,'' he swallowed visibly, his voice turning gruff and tense, ''it may not be yours.''

''Dad, is something wrong?'' Giselle asked, concerned at the strained look on her father's face. The look went beyond long, tedious hours at the office. Much more. Even though Giselle's relationship with her dad was distant at times, she knew him well. Well enough to see all was not right.

Her father sighed, then turned to face her, absently rubbing his hands up and down her arms. Now Giselle was really worried. This display of tenderness was an unaccustomed rarity. With her, he was usually stern, formal, if not downright disapproving.

At his hesitation, Giselle dared to lift a hand to his lined cheek. "Dad?"

"The economy isn't the best, you know. And ... well, sales have been on the decline steadily for the last three years." His arms dropped to his sides, then he turned and walked to the window, his fists shoved deep into the pockets of his trousers.

"I've seen the reports, Dad. We're holding our own. Grant's is one of the few independently owned department stores still making a profit."

"I'd never admit this to your mother, and don't you dare tell her." Over his shoulder, he shot her his typical warning look. "But we've been too conservative in our approach to advertising. Times have changed, Giselle. And I've been too stubborn to see that and change with them." He turned to face her, a sense of urgency giving an edge to his voice. "That's why this new catalog is so important. We've never invested so much in any form of advertising. We've got to show the public that Grant's is a store for *all* the family, from infants to those irritating rapping beeboppers. Not just Mom and Pop."

A feeling of dread mixed with guilt seeped into Giselle. Good Lord, what was she going to do now? She had to find a way to keep her pictures out of that catalog. Her father was sinking money into advertising to increase exposure, but she didn't think her bikini-clad body plastered on every page of the swimsuit section was what he had in mind.

"When do you want to start your vacation?"

His question interrupted her racing thoughts.

"Friday."

"Friday?" he barked, thankfully returning once

again to his normal bossy self. "Don't believe in giving much notice, do you, little lady?"

Feeling as if they had crossed a rare kind of father-daughter threshold, she kissed him on the cheek, then gave him a grin. "That's one of the perks of being the boss's daughter."

When she raced back down to her office, she found Anita waiting. "Well? What did he say?"

"After glaring at me for what seemed like forever, he finally agreed. For a moment, I thought he was going to refuse. Then my butt would've really been in a sling—no, make that a cast; it's already in a sling." Giselle sighed and flopped down in a chair. After rocking back and forth, she leaned her head back and stared at the ceiling. "Oh, Nita, what am I going to do?"

"Simple." Anita shrugged. "Go to the island with Mitch, model—in and out of the bedroom—give your hormones a healthy dose of better-than-chocolate nooki, then come home."

"Who said anything about the bedroom? Regardless of my deprived hormones, that's not part of the bet."

Anita snorted. "The bet? Honey, I was just laying out the perks for you. If it were me, I certainly wouldn't delay getting my hands on that apple-cheeked rump of his. You'd better get a couple of packages of condoms."

"Nita!"

"You know, they come in glow-in-the-dark now."

Speechless, yet wickedly mesmerized by the crazy mental image, all Giselle could do was silently open and close her mouth until she finally found her sanity and her voice. "From the way you're talking, sounds as if *your* hormones are on the endangered list, not mine. Maybe you should go with him."

"Nah," Anita shot back, looking down at her plump legs. "I don't have legs like you. Although I wouldn't mind running around on a tropical island, like Jane with Tarzan chasing after me." She closed her eyes and fluttered her hand against her chest. "Mmmm, Mitch Sullivan in a loincloth. Be still my heart."

Giselle couldn't help but grin. It was indeed a wonderful mental picture. But instead of a loincloth, a white towel came to mind. A very skimpy white towel.

"How long will you be on the island with Tarzan man?"

"The message he left said two weeks, more or less."

"I, uh, I hate to tell you this, but you may not be gone that long. Then again, you may be swept off the face of the earth. Oh, how romantic. To disappear with the man of your dreams," Anita giggled.

"What are you talking about, Anita?"

"While I was in my office, I heard Rainy Day's weather forecast on the radio. Seems there's a tropical wave coming off the coast of Africa, headed for the Caribbean. So instead of Paradise Key, you may end up on Gilligan's island."

"Oh, great." Giselle plopped her chin in her hand. "Just what I need. I have to be gone at least two weeks so you can arrange for another photographer and model to do an identical shoot with the same swimwear."

Anita's eyes widened behind her glasses. "How on earth do you expect me to do that?"

"I have no idea. But you got me into this, now you've got to do something to get me out. That catalog can't come out with my face in it. Have some head shots done. Maybe we can splice them on top of my body pictures.''

"Oh, that ought to be cute.''

"Have you got a better idea? I wouldn't be in this predicament if it weren't for you." Giselle pointed a finger at her friend. "And get that Cheshire-cat grin off of your face!"

If anything, Anita's grin broadened. "My, my, aren't we touchy.''

Leaning forward, Giselle took the stance she had seen her father use many times. "Touchy? Me? What do I have to be touchy about? Well, let's see. I'm going off to an isolated island in the Keys with a man I hardly know—''

"The rest of the camera crew will be down there in a few days and—''

Giselle ignored the interruption. "Doing something that I don't know how to do—''

"You're a natural beauty, don't worry about it.''

"At the beginning of hurricane season with a storm already brewing—''

"You know how unpredictable those storms can be. Odds are it will fizzle out before it even reaches the Keys.''

"And last, but certainly not least, my picture, clad in two tiny strips of cloth, will be all over a catalog for a store owned by *my* father. As soon as he sees it, I'll be running for my life. No. I don't see why I'm so touchy. Can't imagine why, can you?" Giselle's voice had steadily gotten higher in volume and pitch as she leaned closer and closer to Anita. Now she stood on tiptoe, glaring down her nose at her.

Anita shifted in her chair. *"Well!"* she declared. "Maybe touchy isn't the right word.''

* * *

Mitch answered the insistent pounding at the door. "Rockhead, I knew it was you."

Curtis grinned at him. "Ahoy there, little buddy." He plopped a white sailor hat down on Mitch's head and started whistling the theme from *Gilligan's Island.*

Mitch felt his lips twitch. It was hard to stay mad at Curtis. Although crude, he was also a live wire, unpredictable, and downright incorrigible. Mitch had to admit that was what had drawn him to the big guy in the first place.

"So I hear you're going to be swinging in a hammock with the luscious Ginger."

Mitch closed the door. "How did you know?"

"Don't you know, I heard it through the grapevine," Curtis began singing as he twirled his larger-than-life body around the room.

"Cool it. You're not exactly a California Raisin, you know," Mitch said, shaking his head. He took off the silly hat and dropped it onto the couch. "I'd say you're more like an overripe prune."

"Speaking of which, I had a whole bowlful for breakfast. Want to hear?" Curtis had stopped his dancing, a mischievous grin split his face. "Hey, let's turn on some music. I think rap is the rhythm I'm looking for."

In spite of himself, Mitch laughed. "I've got to pack. You do what you want." He started to leave the room, but stopped. "Anything but *that.*"

"Party pooper. Want some help packing?"

"Yeah, right. No thank you. I don't want any rubber spiders or snakes jumping out at me when I open my suitcase. Besides, I've just about finished. I'm packing the camera equipment now."

Large steel cases were set about the room, each one carefully labeled.

Curtis glanced around. "Man, look at all this stuff. You certainly don't pack light, do you, little buddy? Hell, I can get by with just a pillowcaseful. And that'll last me three weeks."

Mitch gestured to the cases. "Most of this is equipment."

"Oh, yeah. That's right. You're going to be on a private island. Clothes aren't necessary. You can run around naked if you want." Curtis leaned over and lowered his voice. "But make sure you put on plenty of sunscreen down in *man's-land.*" He pointed downward.

"Man's-land?"

"The old amusement park between the legs. Believe you me, you don't want to get *that* sunburned. 'Cause if it starts peeling, you'll never get a woman. They'll think you've got leprosy."

"Rockhead, don't you have anything better to do?" Mitch asked in exasperation. He liked his friend, but Curtis in small doses was about all he could handle.

"What? What did I say this time?"

"As always, it was good to see you, Curtis." Mitch took him by one beefy arm and walked him to the door.

"Need a lift to the airport tomorrow?"

"Only if you can be on time. My plane leaves for Miami at ten."

"Okay. Sure. No problem." Curtis opened the door and squinted until his eyes were slits. "Let me give you some advice, Grasshopper."

Mitch smothered a grin.

"Watch out for voodoo. It's rampant in the islands. You might come back with a hex on you. And the

hex might be love." He broke out in some silly love
song, the words ludicrous, the melody off-key.

Mitch watched the lumbering, retreating figure
and wondered if Curtis had a serious bone in his
body. If he did, Mitch had never seen it in the ten
years he'd known him.

He closed the door and went back to packing the
camera equipment. The only thing he wanted to
bring back from the Keys was a stack of dynamite
proofs of Giselle. And with a model like her, he didn't
see how he could miss.

Excitement sizzled through him. He wasn't sure if
it stemmed from the fact that he was starting a new
shoot, perhaps the biggest of his career; or if it was
from the thought of seeing Giselle again. Or maybe
a little of both.

Mitch couldn't think of a situation that could be
better than spending long summer days down in the
Florida Keys doing something he loved with a beautiful woman whose dark jade eyes and long legs sent
his heartbeats off the scale. Yes, the next two weeks
could be very interesting. Not to mention stimulating,
in more ways than one. Glancing down in the direction of 'man's-land,' he shrugged and tossed a tube
of sunscreen into his duffel bag.

Giant windows lined the airport corridor. Giselle
paced the floor and glanced out the window for the
umpteenth time.

"Will you sit down? You're making me a nervous
wreck," Anita huffed. "He'll be here. Don't worry."

Checking her watch, Giselle looked at the line of
passengers already boarding the flight. "Our flight
leaves in ten minutes. *Ten!*"

"G.G., he has his ticket and seating assignment,

right next to you, I might add. So don't worry. Go ahead and get in line. I'll watch for him." Anita stood and gave her a quick hug. "Have a good time, and stop acting so nervous. You'll get the hiccups again. I'll take care of everything on this end. You just hold up your end of it and we'll have smooth sailing."

"How do you expect me to get him to ask me out on a date on the island? There's nothing there but sand, palm trees and water."

"You'll think of something. And if you fail, remember, I'll take that in large bills."

"Don't remind me. Are you sure—?"

Anita took her by the shoulders, twirled her around and gave her a little shove. "Now go, before you wear a hole in the carpet."

Giselle got in line and smiled blankly at the person ahead of her. Her nerves were stretched tighter than a rubber band on a windup toy. And she feared the moment she laid eyes on Mitch Sullivan again, the band would let loose and she'd whirl around in a never-ending circle like an out of control Energizer Bunny.

Control. Somehow, she had to maintain control. After all, for the next two weeks she would be with Mitch, day and night. And that was what bothered her. During the days, the shoots and business would occupy their time. But she knew better than anyone about the nights. She'd spent many hours on Paradise Key, and she remembered all too well how the soft breezes and the endless star-filled night sky could create an ambiance of romance.

She could only hope she and her man-starved hormones wouldn't get caught up in the magic of it all. Then again, a little part of her couldn't help but hope that maybe the magic would rub off on Mitch as well.

* * *

"Rockhead, I told you my plane left at ten, not that I wanted to get here at ten!" Mitch snapped at Curtis as they ran down the airport corridor. "I just hope I haven't missed it altogether."

"I, uh," Curtis gasped, "I'd have something to say to that, little buddy, but I'm . . . out of breath."

Mitch glanced at him. Red in the face from exertion, Curtis lumbered and rolled down the aisle like a huge elephant in a stampede. The crowds of people took one look at him and parted, getting out of his way as quickly as possible.

"Look, there's my gate." Mitch pointed.

"Thank you, Lord." Curtis rolled his eyes heavenward.

The two ran to the lady at the booth just as the last person disappeared down the long hall that carried the passengers to the airplane.

"Where the hell have you been?" a voice demanded behind him.

Curtis slid a glance to the woman who stood next to him with hands on her hips. "Hey, cuz. We were running just a tad late. Had trouble getting through the metal detector. You know, I never realized brass knuckles were illegal."

While Mitch checked in, his gaze wandered to the woman Curtis had called 'cuz.' Something about her was familiar, but he couldn't quite place where he'd seen her before. He cleared his throat and elbowed his friend in the back.

Curtis turned around. "What?"

"Are you going to introduce me or not?"

"Uh, well . . . you don't have time, little buddy," Curtis stammered as he pushed Mitch toward the gate. "You have a plane to catch, and you're late enough as it is. You wouldn't want to keep that gorgeous babe waiting, now would you? Have a nice trip and if you happen to see the Professor and Mary Ann, tell them hello."

Mitch grabbed his carry-on bag from Curtis and headed down the corridor. He glanced over his shoulder to see Curtis give the woman in the glasses a high-five.

Puzzled, Mitch ran the rest of the way down the hall and scooted onto the plane moments before the door closed. It didn't take him long to find Giselle. She sat on the last aisle in the first-class section, staring daggers at him.

He stowed his bag in the rack above their row, flopped down in the seat and gave her a lopsided grin. "Hello, Legs."

"Where the hell have you been?" she hissed.

"What is that? Phrase of the day? I just heard those same words from some lady with glasses and a smart mouth at the gate."

Giselle fell silent. Her green eyes widened, a pink flush stained her cheeks. "Anita," she muttered.

A funny-sounding squeak escaped her lips, and her shoulders jumped.

"Are you okay?" He leaned toward her, straining to hear her answer over the roar of the engines as they prepared for rollback.

She raised her voice. "It's nothing." *Hiccup.* "I'm fine."

"Have you got the hiccups, Legs?"

Hiccup. "I'm afraid so. I get them when I'm nervous." She bent down and searched through her large purse.

"I'll get you some water—"

"Don't bother," she told him as she produced a small jar of peanut butter.

He watched her dip a slender finger into the nutty spread and pop some into her mouth. His loins tightened as her lips closed around the tip of her finger. And he suddenly wished it was his finger in her warm mouth, with her soft lips taking him in, licking, twirling her tongue around and around.

Automatically, and knowing that he shouldn't, his body followed his thoughts. He reached over, swirled a finger in the jar and held it out to her. Her eyes widened with surprise, her pink lips trembled. Before she had the chance to refuse, and he had the chance to rethink what he was doing, Mitch touched his finger to her lips and delved inside her mouth. Just as he thought, her lips closing around his finger sent a jolt of desire through him that made him hard, instantly ready.

She released his finger, and he slowly pulled it from her mouth, tenderly tracing her lips. Then he slid the same finger into his own mouth. He closed his eyes for a brief moment as her taste mingled with his own. When he glanced back at her, Giselle's gazed was fixed on his mouth.

"Are your hiccups all gone?" he asked, his face just inches from hers.

Her eyes turned to dark liquid emeralds as they lifted to meet his. Her voice barely above a husky whisper, she answered, "Ah, yes, thank you." She pulled away, put the lid back on the jar and returned it to her purse.

He grinned at her. "You know, Legs, there's nothing to be nervous about. Flying is a breeze."

The plane taxied down the runway, then gathered speed as it finally left the ground. Mitch reached over and covered the delicate hand that gripped the arm rest. She looked at him in surprise, but didn't protest.

He gave her a reassuring smile and tucked her hand into the crook of his arm.

"It's okay, honey. Everything will be fine. Remember, we're flying into Paradise."

Chapter Five

Steam rose from the wet asphalt runway. The sun streamed down, heating the lush vegetation that surrounded the tiny airstrip. The afternoon shower that had bathed the island earlier created a humid tropical steam bath.

Giselle lifted her hair off her neck and wiped at the sweat trickling down the sides of her face. She pulled at the white silk blouse that clung to her perspiring body like a second skin. Geez, she felt like a wilted flower on a soggy prom corsage.

She looked over at Mitch as he and the pilot unloaded supplies and luggage from the small airplane. Irritation hit her. Mitch still looked fresh and clean. That figures, she thought. Mr. Perfect had his act together, while she was a basket case of frazzled nerves.

Her nervousness had nothing to do with the fear of flying as he had presumed. Countless times she'd traveled the same remote route, in a puddle jumper smaller than the Cessna that now stood on the tarmac. One stroke of luck had come her way today: her father's usual pilot, Lee, was on vacation. Although she hadn't seen him in years, he was sure to have recognized her and blown the whole thing.

As for the rest of the day, the closer they had come

to the island, the more peanut butter she had consumed. Now she felt bloated, even a bit queasy. If she didn't watch it, she'd be in no shape to fit into any of the swimsuits.

After the last box was unloaded from the plane, Mitch said a few words to the pilot, then turned to Giselle. A wide grin split his face and his indigo eyes danced.

What the hell was that all about?

As she watched the pilot get into the airplane and take off, she swallowed hard. Now they were alone. Really alone. At least for the next few days until the rest of the crew arrived.

Giselle squelched the urge to run after the plane, grab on to the wing and plead with the pilot to take her back to Miami. But she couldn't do that. Right now, thanks to Anita and the blasted bet, she was stuck here. But instead of having Gilligan for company, she was stranded with Tarzan. A damned devastatingly dimpled Tarzan.

Mitch walked over to her, his gait unhurried, his hips swinging lazily. He reminded her of a big tomcat, sure of his territory, sure of his prey. And she felt like a helpless myna bird who'd lost its voice as the huge mesmerizing cat approached. One thing was certain, he'd better not try to mark her as his own, or by God, she'd pluck every one of those whiskers out one by one. Giselle gave herself a mental shake, and the long whiskers vanished from Mitch's face. But so help her, if he meowed or hissed, she'd take off running.

Get a grip, G.G. It's been a long day, and you're losing it. The thought jolted her out of her hair-raising fantasy. She felt almost foolish as he began to speak, no *me-Tarzan, you-Jane* grunts, no tomcat meow, but a normal human sound after all.

"Ready to go, Legs?" he asked, looking around.

"There ought to be some kind of vehicle around here somewhere to get us up to the house."

"Yes, over there." She pointed to a small metal building at the edge of the runway.

He shot her a sharp look, his blue eyes probing her face. "How do you know?"

Too late, Giselle realized her slip. She was going to have to be very careful not to reveal her knowledge of the island and its facilities. "I, well, I guess that's where it would be. I don't know for sure, but it's a place to start looking."

If possible, her perspiration level rose a notch as Mitch continued to stare her down. The smile suddenly returned to his face, and relief cascaded through her.

"Not only great legs, but smart, too."

The relief short-lived, her nerves stretched to the limit, Giselle bristled at his words. "What a sexist thing to say! Don't mistake me for an airhead, buddy." Indignation drew Giselle's shoulders back and her head up. Smart, huh? Hell, if he only knew. And right now, by God, she'd love to tell him about her degree in marketing, not to mention that her *real* job had nothing whatsoever to do with her body, and *everything* to do with her brain.

The smile slipped from his face. "Don't get so uptight, honey. Take it as it was meant. A compliment, that's all." He stalked away from her, but not before she heard him mutter, "Women."

Remember the bet, you fool. This was not the way to go about accomplishing the goal, she reminded herself. She was supposed to woo him, get him to date her, not put him on the defensive.

"Mitch! Wait," she called. With her long stride, she caught up with him and laid a hand on his arm.

"I'm sorry. I'm hot, sweaty and grouchy. I shouldn't be taking it out on you."

He continued to walk toward the shed, his eyes focused forward. "You've got that right, Legs. If you've got PMS, you could have warned me."

"What?"

A devilish, all-knowing, infuriatingly male grin spread across his face. "If that's your problem, then I've got the perfect solution." His sapphire eyes raked over her body, his voice lowered to a seductive murmur. "Believe me, it works every time." Blond eyebrows wagged at her, then he gave her a wicked wink.

It was her turn to stalk off. Embarrassment and anger flooded through her. All afternoon, Mitch had been the ultimate gentleman, but now, he had returned to his usual prehistoric, arrogant self. She called over her shoulder, "For your information, I don't have PMS."

"Could have fooled me."

"Let's just find the Jeep and get to the house."

Together, they turned the corner and walked into the shed. Once again, Mitch's gaze bore into her, his expression suspicious.

"How did you know there was a *Jeep* in here?"

Dammit, Giselle. Watch your tongue. And for heaven's sake, think fast!

"Don't you ever go to the movies? There are always Jeeps on these islands in films. Besides, the last shoot I was on, we were on an island just like this, and as a matter of fact, we all drove Jeeps." It amazed Giselle how easy the little lies seemed to have become. Boy, could she give old Pinocchio a run for his money— Anita would be so proud. As for herself, she felt like a heel. Well, if this whole thing blew up on her, maybe she could sign with the Barnum and Bailey Circus as a stand-in for the elephant show.

"Oh yeah? Then tell me, Legs, what else do you know about the Keys?" he asked, his hands on his hips, his look one of disbelief.

With a mask of confidence she didn't quite feel, she commented, "There's usually only one road that goes all the way around an island as small as this. So, lucky for you, since there's no one to ask for directions, not that you would since you're a man and all, we shouldn't get lost."

No comment greeted her, but his eyes blazed blue fire. They jumped in the Jeep and Mitch turned the key. After several tries, the engine still wouldn't start. The heat in the tin building was stifling, and sweat trickled down her already soaked blouse. Giselle's patience was slipping. She knew how to start this stubborn vehicle, but did she dare? She'd already revealed too much about the island. If she slipped up any more, he was sure to call her bluff. But after he'd tried two more times, she couldn't stand it anymore.

"Mitch, I hate to threaten your masculinity, but for God's sake, if we're going to make it to the bungalow anytime today, let me try my luck at starting this thing."

One blond brow arched over one furious eye. "Are you sure you don't have PMS?"

She gave him a black look.

"Okay, have at it, Legs." He settled back in the seat and crossed his arms.

A tiny bit of satisfaction spread through her when she noticed Mitch had begun to sweat as well. No more Mr. Perfect. She wasn't the only one who looked wilted beyond repair.

Giselle reached over and jiggled the ignition. "Pump the gas." She waited until his foot pressed down on the pedal several times, then she jimmied the key again, before twisting it all the way around. The Jeep started on the first try.

Triumphant, she looked up at him and found his face so close to hers, she could see the indigo circle surrounding the sapphire irises of his eyes. For a breath of a moment, neither spoke, her voice all but forgotten as she lost herself in the fathomless depths of his gaze.

Mitch snaked out a hand to cup the back of her head, bringing her face even with his, before pressing a soft kiss onto lips that quickly parted in surprise. His mouth left hers, and for just a split second, the expression so brief she could have imagined it, Giselle thought she saw shock tighten his face and widen his eyes. But at his nonchalant words, she knew the fleeting look of surprise had to have been her imagination running wild.

"I can hardly wait to see what other talents you have, honey," he told her, his voice husky yet teasing. "Like I said, gorgeous legs plus brains. What a combination."

Before she could object to his actions, or beg for more, Mitch put the Jeep in reverse, then shifted to drive and headed for the supplies that sat on the side of the runway.

With everything loaded, the Jeep bounced over the rough grassy field toward the only road on the island. The sun beat down, the ocean breeze whipped and tossed Giselle's hair about her head. She gathered it into a ponytail and held it with the hand that still trembled from the surprising kiss. A kiss that left her craving more, yet at the same time left her fearful of the feeling it invoked. Especially since Mitch appeared to be completely unaffected, except for that one moment when she thought she'd seen her own surprise at his actions mirrored in his eyes. Her imagination? Wishful hormonal thinking? Or something more?

He drove the twisted road with care. The long tanned fingers of one hand loosely controlled the wheel, the other hand rested on the gear shift. Those cool, delicious fingers had once run through her hair, she remembered. Giselle's gaze traveled up his muscled arms to his face. And now, those smooth, purposeful lips had kissed hers. God, what more would come? Could she resist the attraction to him? She couldn't get too involved. She had to remember that. Being with him was only the result of a careless bet. Somehow she had to keep that in mind. If her deprived hormones had anything to say about it, that task might prove to be downright impossible.

"Why did you do that?" she blurted out, then immediately wished she could take the words back. But she had to know.

He slid a glance to her. "Do what, Legs?"

Her face flamed, and it wasn't because of the burning sun. "You know . . . *that,* back there in the shed."

"You had a problem, and I had the solution." A slow grin curved the corners of his mouth. "I told you, it works every time."

A thousand retorts came to mind, but Giselle couldn't manage to squeak one out. The only sound that escaped her lips was a strangled choke.

The slow grin turned to a broad, dimpled smile and a wink. "Peanut butter, anyone?"

The Grant bungalow stood with its red tiled roof and sun-bleached stucco walls on a crest overlooking a sugary sand beach. A covered verandah circled the entire perimeter of the sprawling structure. The lawn surrounding the house was lush and thick with deep green grass, tropical flowers of every kind, color and fragrance, and towering palm trees.

Mitch pulled the Jeep into the circular drive and stopped in front of the main entrance. "Wow, this isn't a bungalow, it's a mansion."

Giselle pried her eyes away from the familiar summer home that had been the place of so many hours of enjoyment, and looked at Mitch. "What did you expect? Gilligan's island? A grass hut with dirt floors, maybe?"

A sheepish, yet totally charming look crossed his face. "I guess I should have known better, huh? Old man Grant never does anything halfway."

"You've got that right," she mumbled.

"What was that?"

"Um, I said, that's what I've heard. If his stores are any indication, then I wouldn't expect anything less than this." She pointed back to the bungalow.

The urge to jump out of the Jeep and run inside was almost irresistible. The caretakers had outdone themselves, she thought, as she looked at the perfectly manicured lawn and the flower gardens that bordered the estate. And right now, even though she hadn't ventured inside the house, she could almost imagine the familiar childhood smells, a combination of fruit, coconut and the potent blossoms of plumeria.

Unable to resist any longer, Giselle slid from the Jeep and walked up the stairs that led to the verandah and the front door. Lovingly, she traced the railing of the porch, where she'd sat for hour upon hour, reading, daydreaming and talking with her mother. She tipped a few white wicker rocking chairs and looked back at Mitch.

"Well, are you going to sit out in that Jeep all day or are you coming in?"

For what seemed like ages, Mitch sat and looked

at her. Finally, he joined her on the verandah. "I think I just found the first place for the shoot." Excitement filled his voice. "You look so at home here, with your long dark hair and mysterious island eyes. I can picture you sitting on that railing, with one foot swinging, wearing one of those filmy cover-ups."

Giselle almost choked. For the umpteenth time, warning bells went off in her head. She had to remember to keep her love for this island and this home to herself. She hadn't been aware her feelings were that evident. Apparently, Mitch was quick to read her expressions. Then again, that was his job.

"In fact, let me dig my camera out right now." He turned and sprinted down the stairs.

"Whoa, hold on there, Mr. Snappy. I'm hot, tired and more than ready for a nice cool shower. I feel like a melted chocolate bar—"

Mitch sniffed the air. "More like a Reese's Peanut Butter Cup." He grinned up at her.

She could see that he wasn't about to let her live down her peanut butter habit. However, too tired and sticky to do anything but think of a shower and nice cool sheets under her weary body as she took a short nap, she did not take the bait he offered.

"Surely we can wait until tomorrow to take some pictures. Can't we at least unpack first?"

He debated a few moments. "Okay, honey. You can have today off. But tomorrow, from the first morning light to sunset, we're going to scout every inch of this island and map out the best backdrops for the shoots—and the best lighting. I want everything to be ready when the rest of the crew arrives. Although," he added, looking around, "I'm in no hurry to leave this paradise." He slowly walked back up the stairs and took a few steps until he stood just a hairsbreadth away from her. "I mean, you never know what might happen when the magic of the island invades your veins."

Mitch dug in his pocket, fished out a key and opened the door. With a wink and a flash of a devilish dimple, he walked into the house ahead of Giselle, leaving her outside experiencing a mixture of hope and dread. Hope that the magic of Paradise Key would indeed creep into him. Dread that the very same magic would steal her heart.

After unloading the many boxes of equipment, supplies and luggage, Mitch took Giselle's advice and opted for a cool shower. But for him, a nap was out of the question. Too many thoughts swirled around in his head. The first and foremost being of Giselle.

He wandered out on the verandah that faced the beach. The water below changed from translucent aqua, where it spilled onto the beach, to a deeper green that highlighted the coral reefs beneath. Then finally, yards beyond the reef, a dark sapphire hinted at the ocean's immeasurable bottom.

Flinging himself into one of the wooden-slat beach chairs, Mitch debated what he had done that afternoon. Something impulsive and not at all smart, that's what. He couldn't believe he'd kissed her. He hadn't planned to. But regardless, he had. And the feelings that one little kiss had stirred in him were surprising and terrifying, even now.

Oh, he had tried to pass it off as nothing, but still, hours later, his heart pounded. His groin tightened when he thought of how sweet and soft Giselle's lips had felt under his. He had wanted to kiss her again. Deeper. Longer. And judging from her response, that wouldn't have been a problem.

But sirens had gone off in his head that warned

him to pull back. He didn't know what it was, but Giselle was different. Already, she had become more to him than just another model. Her emerald eyes pulled at some deep, hidden chamber of his heart. The way her hair blew about her head made him want to once again thread his fingers through the strands, to feel its silkiness, its sun-spun warmth. And now that he had tasted her, he craved even more.

Maintaining a professional distance, at least until after the final shoot, had to be his first priority. If he didn't, he knew he wouldn't be at his best. And neither would she.

Giselle was unlike any woman he'd ever met. And even though he had only scratched the surface of her personality, instinctively he knew she wouldn't be happy with just a one-night stand or a quick fling for the next two weeks. She'd been too surprised by his kiss. No, Miss Legs wasn't used to kissing strangers or to casual love play.

And yet, that's all Mitch could ever be to her. A lover in the physical sense. The rest of him, including his heart, had to stay remote. Aloof. He didn't need the complications of a relationship. With Celeste, he'd seen firsthand how this so-called love could mess up your life. And he was bound and determined it would never happen to him again, no matter how beautiful Giselle was or how soft and tempting and inviting her lips were. No matter how silky and long and luscious her legs were. No matter how her sparkling emerald green eyes mesmerized him . . .

Even though he'd left Curtis in Houston, it was almost as if his friend's irritating influence was egging Mitch to go for it. A part of him really wanted to. Especially the man's-land part. But a bigger part feared involvement, completely destroying the rising amusement park between his legs. Mitch wasn't sure

which part would win—the bullet ride or the tunnel
of love. Hell, he wasn't sure which part he *wanted* to
win. Or even if he had control over either one, he
thought as he looked down. That was the scariest
part. That and knowing he was thinking too much
like Curtis. God help him, he feared he'd left any
form of control, not to mention common sense, back
in Houston.

Giselle awoke slowly, yawning, stretching. A smile
curved the corners of her mouth. She felt refreshed,
rested, and she was at her home away from home.
The late afternoon sun streamed through the wooden
shutters that covered one entire side of the room,
the windows, even the sliding glass door. A wall of glass
lined every room in the back of the house, affording a
panoramic view of where the Gulf of Mexico met the
Atlantic Ocean.

Like a contented kitty, she stretched again. This
island had to be one of her favorite places on earth.
It had been too long since she'd been here. Way too
long. But now she was here for vacation, for some
sun, and fun . . .

She shot upright in bed. *Mitch.* Yeah, it had been
too long since she had relaxed here on Paradise Key,
all right. However, this time she wasn't with her family.
And she wasn't here for a vacation. She was here to
work at a job she knew nothing about, with a man
who sent her emotions into a whirlwind. Relax around
Mitch? Yeah, right. And she'd kick peanut butter,
cold turkey.

Scooting out of the king-sized bed, Giselle slipped
on a pair of white shorts and a dark green tank top,
then folded back the shutters. She brushed her tan-

gled still-damp hair into a loose ponytail, dabbed on some lipstick, and headed out to find Mitch.

It didn't take long. She spotted him on the far corner of the verandah, stretched out in a hammock with an arm flung over his eyes. She shook her head and smiled. So much for Tarzan the macho man not needing a nap. The afternoons were so blazing hot and hazy, he would soon find they weren't much good for anything but a snooze.

Her gaze swept over him, and a thrill of enjoyment at watching him while he was unaware and unguarded sent her hormones into a dither. He had changed into a pair of frayed, cuttoff shorts, his torso left temptingly bare. A fine dusting of golden hair swirled over smooth muscle and tendon. Much to her dismay, her breath quickened. While she had seen his bare chest before, the sight started a tiny flame inside her. The flame spiraled downward until it settled into a warm glow in her most feminine depths.

Trying to squelch the aching warmth, she wrenched her hungry eyes away from his sinewy chest up to his face, partially covered by one muscled forearm. Her eyes feasted on his firm, yet generous mouth, flanked by a set of deep, charming dimples. A warm, wet mouth that just a few hours ago had captured hers in a brief but heart-melting kiss. Thick blond hair, although shorter than it had been a few days ago, still brushed his shoulders. All he needed was a black patch over one eye and a parrot perched on his shoulder to complete the image of an island pirate.

Oh, great, Giselle. First a big tomcat, then Tarzan and now the image of a pirate. The cool shower and the nap were supposed to have done away with those ridiculous thoughts.

Her stomach rumbled as a loud reminder that she hadn't had anything to eat but peanut butter in hours.

As long as it didn't require gourmet expertise, she didn't mind doing her fair share of the cooking. However, there was no way she'd let him treat her like the "little woman." Since there was no staff, the housework would be divided up equally, whether he liked it or not. And if his arrogant Fred Flintstone manner was any indication, Giselle feared he would expect her to be just like Wilma and do it all.

Just the thought of his arrogance gave her an irresistible urge to go and tip over the hammock. But she didn't have the chance. Mitch turned over in his sleep, and deposited himself on the deck with a thump.

He awoke with a start and rubbed his banged forehead. "What the hell?"

Laughing, Giselle walked over, looked down at him and crossed her arms. "Sleep much? You know, a roll over in a hammock can be tricky." She shook her head, then tapped one finger against her lips. "I thought waking you gently was best, but this works for me."

She reached out a hand to help him up. "I'm starving."

Mitch took her hand and climbed to his feet. Even in his bare feet, he still stood a few inches taller than Giselle. Now that she had to look up at him, her bravado slipped a bit.

A sexy grin spread across his face as he held her hand, his thumb tracing patterns over her palm. Then he commented, his voice husky from sleep, yet so suggestive, "I'm starving, too. Shall we get to cooking?"

Giselle's reply stuck in her throat, and she pressed down the urge to hiccup.

"In the kitchen, I mean."

The pent-up breath she'd been holding, seeped

out through pursed lips. "Oh, yes, of course, the kitchen."

One arrogant eyebrow rose over one teasing sapphire eye. "Unless you had something else in mind, honey."

Words failed her. Worry and fear hit her like a dousing of ice water. Good God, were her desperate hormones thumping around so loudly he could hear? Were her feelings that transparent? No, they couldn't be. Because she had no idea what she felt about this man in the first place. Besides, cave-man arrogance practically oozed from his every pore. How could she possibly want him? She couldn't, she told herself.

Yeah, right, and birds don't fly and hormones don't exist.

Mitch squeezed her hand. "Well?"

Giselle blinked and snatched her hand back. Then she turned and called over her shoulder, "The kitchen is this way."

"Chicken," he uttered in a soft, but challenging voice.

As she stalked off, his chuckle followed her. The urge to turn right back around and offer him her own challenge—a good swift kick right where it was sure to hurt—nearly overwhelmed her.

For Giselle, the rest of the night was indeed a challenge. Mitch's eyes followed her every move, his warm presence always just inches away. The bungalow, the verandah, even the beach seemed too intimate. The magic of the tropical night seemed to invade her thoughts, even the very breaths she inhaled. And with the magic, there was Mitch. Everywhere she went, he was there, filling her up with his closeness, his essence.

And every time he looked at her with those mesmerizing eyes and that dimpled grin, it was a private, silent reminder of the kiss they'd shared that afternoon. Giselle felt the urge to prove him right by giving him a few clucks. Yep, she was chicken, all right. But somehow, she had to get over it. She had a bet to win. And no amount of clucking would get her out of it.

Chapter Six

Click, click, click.

The same irritating noise seeped into Giselle's dreamless sleep. She shifted restlessly, willing the sound away.

Click, click . . . click, click.

This time the repetitive noise sounded closer to her ear. Slowly, she peeped through one eye. For a moment, the world seemed fuzzy, in a haze. Then she focused in on the source of the sound. Her eyes flew open, and she bolted upright in the bed. At the very last second, she remembered to snatch the sheet up to cover her bare breasts.

"What in the hell are you doing?" she demanded, her voice still husky from sleep.

Click, click.

"What does it look like I'm doing? I'm working," Mitch answered as he walked to the closed shutters and folded them back. The soft glow of dawn chased the shadows from the room. "Remember what I told you yesterday?" He looked back at her with shrewd eyes. "Perfect. Hold it right there."

Click.

"First morning light, we start to work."

Giselle looked out of the glass doors. Hues of pale azure blue and pink reflected off the glistening waves.

"For heaven's sake, Mitch, it's barely daylight." One hand clutched the sheet, the other raked through her tangled hair.

"It's been dawn for nearly an hour, Legs." He aimed his camera at her again and snapped off several shots in a row.

"Would you stop? I thought this was a swimsuit layout," she protested, suddenly feeling shy, if not downright inadequate. "You know *swimsuit*, not *birthday suit.*"

"I thought I'd get some skin shots first."

That was a line of bull if she had ever heard one.

He peered over the lens, a devilish look dancing in his deep blue eyes. "Besides, there's nothing more sexy than a woman right when she wakes up . . . with her hair scattered wildly about her shoulders, her eyes still heavy and seductive with sleep . . . her smell musky and soft."

Giselle's gaze followed him as he walked to the other side of the bed where the view of the ocean faced him. His voice was warm and low and coaxing, his words left her breathless, almost wanting. *Almost, like hell.* More like definitely, unequivocally wanting. She found herself speechless, and she hated that most of all. She should tell him to get the hell out of her room. After all, she only worked for him and still had a right to her privacy. In fact, she should pitch a royal fit for his rude intrusion. Yes, that's what she *should* do. But she wouldn't, unless she really wanted to convince him she had a permanent case of PMS.

Click, click, click, click.

Of course, if she weren't such a chicken, she could take advantage of the situation and use it to win the bet. But as it was, she seemed frozen in place. She wanted to fling the sheet over her head and hide, but his next words not only froze her but encased her in ice.

"But this ... I must say, this is an added bonus. It's not every day you find a woman with all of those early morning sensual qualities, but with a little something extra." He lowered the camera and gave her a smile that was wicked, manly and irritatingly arrogant all at the same time. "Sleeping in the nude. I would never have guessed."

The sheet clenched in fists tucked under her chin, Giselle sent him what she hoped was a go-straight-to-hell-do-not-pass-go look. Last night, she knew she should have slipped on a T-shirt or something. But even after the sun had set, the air had been moist, heavy and still, and the thought of sleeping with anything tangled around her sweaty body was out of the question. However, now she regretted her actions, the more so with every passing second that Mitch stared at her, his eyes stripping away the thin sheet.

His grin broadened as heat burned her face. A blush not only caused by embarrassment, but by a simmering anger that had begun to boil. Just who did he think he was, barging in here uninvited?

Your boss for the next few weeks, and the answer to the bet.

Click.

"I agreed to model swimwear for you, not bedclothes," she bit out through clenched teeth. "Now, if you don't mind, I'd like to get out of bed and get dressed."

Once again he lowered his camera. "No, I don't mind at all. In fact, I'd enjoy it. Go right ahead."

Giselle pointed to the door and the sheet almost slipped through her fingers. Mitch's eyes widened and twinkled with silent laughter at her frantic actions.

Hiccup. "Out!" *Hiccup.* If possible, her face burned even hotter. Oh, God, here we go again.

Blond eyebrows arched over bright blue eyes, the dimples in his cheeks deepened. "Okay, Legs, you win. Be ready in five minutes. Breakfast is on me . . . this morning."

Hiccup.

"I'd ask you what you prefer, but—"

Hiccup.

"—I presume you want peanut butter."

Mitch pored over the map of the island he had found earlier that morning in the study/communications room. Although roughly drawn, it would still be a big help in finding the best possible places for the shoots.

He looked up as Giselle walked into the room wearing white cutoff shorts and a white scooped-neck top. Her dark hair hung in loose waves. Her face glowed with just the right touch of makeup.

This morning, he'd gone to her room with the innocent intention of waking her, and *only* that. However, when she hadn't responded to his light knock, Mitch had peeked in on her. Not one of his smartest moves. Sensuality oozed from this woman, even in her sleep. And the want he'd been fighting for days had nearly overtaken him.

The photographer in him couldn't resist capturing her pure sensuality with the camera. Even when she woke up, the array of emotions that had crossed her face gave him just a glimpse of the woman inside. The real Giselle—sexy, desirable, intelligent, captivating, vulnerable. All woman. *A sweet Texas lady.*

He pushed the thought away. But he couldn't force the image aside, not that he really wanted to . . . Her

naked body covered by a thin sheet, the sleepy look
in her eyes, the huskiness of her low voice. Even
though she'd been livid—which had only added to
her beauty—he'd still wanted her, still ached for her.

It had taken every bit of his self-control to walk
out of that room without kissing her, touching her,
without pressing her back down onto the soft, massive
bed and possessing her sweet body. And now, looking
up at her as she stood across from him with her hands
on her hips, that same desire seized him once again.

Her voice interrupted his thoughts. "You call this
breakfast?" She gestured to the table.

Mitch glanced at the bowls of cold cereal, the plate
of fresh ripe bananas, and the pot of coffee. "What
did you expect, eggs Benedict? Besides, I thought
models had to watch their weight."

She pulled out a chair and sat down. "I'm not like
most mod—"

"You can say that again," he broke in. "Oh, that
reminds me." He got up from his chair, rummaged
in the cabinet, and with a teasing grin, sat back down.
"I almost forgot the most important thing . . . peanut
butter. It's the damnedest thing, the cabinet is full
of it."

"Give it a rest, would you? Besides, my hiccups are
gone, thank you." Giselle poured milk over the cereal
and sliced a banana into the bowl. Looking over to
his side of the table, she pointed. "What's that?"

"It's a map of the island." Mitch shifted it around
so she could see it.

Milk sloshed out of her bowl. The spoon clattered
to the table. "Where . . . uh, where did you find the
map?" she asked, her eyes wide with an emotion that
almost resembled fear.

"There's a room down the hall." He pointed to
the doorway on the other side of the kitchen. "It's

an office with a shortwave radio in it. The map was tacked up on the wall."

Hiccup. "What else is in that room?" Giselle grabbed the jar of peanut butter and dipped a finger into it.

"What are you nervous about this time?" With arms crossed, he leaned back and stared at her.

"Who says I'm nervous?" *Hiccup.*

"You just did, Miss Hiccup. Come on. Tell me, why does this map make you so nervous?" As quick as a striking snake, he whipped out a hand and grabbed her wrist.

"It doesn't." Giselle fought his grip. "What bothers me is that you snooped around in a home that belongs to someone else," she insisted.

"Good God, Legs, I didn't snoop. The map was in plain sight. Besides, I thought I'd leave the snooping to you. I know you women like to do those sort of things." He turned the map back around.

"Cut the sexist remarks, thank you, and let go of my hand. My cereal is getting soggy," she sniped. Her eyes flashed like lightning illuminating the jungle in a midnight storm.

His lips curved in a grin, and he let go of her wrist. "Well, we can't have that, now can we?"

A half-hour later, Giselle helped Mitch load two bags of camera equipment into the Jeep. As she hoisted herself onto the seat, he flung the map on her lap.

"I'll drive, you navigate." He slid the key into the ignition, went through the steps Giselle had yesterday, and started the Jeep on the first try. A triumphant, dimpled grin split his face. "What can I say? I'm a fast learner."

Mitch's smile sent her pulse racing, even though she willed her emotions to remain calm, neutral. He wasn't the only one who was a fast learner. Much too quickly, she had discovered there was no way to prevent her heart from pounding, her thoughts from scattering when he was around. If she wasn't totally speechless, she was gasping from the blasted hiccups.

Time and time again, her brain urged her to get a grip, but it seemed her body ignored the command. All she could do was stare at him, at his mouth, his cute dimples, the way the wind tousled his thick sun-bleached hair.

At her continued silence, he gestured to the map. "You can read a map, can't you?"

His male condescension brought her out of her reverie. "Of course I can," she retorted. Did he think reading a map was reserved for the male species or something? Little did he know, she had no need for the map. Every nook and cranny of this island, from its sandy shores, to the lush green hills of the mangrove jungle had been committed to memory long ago. The hard task at hand would be to keep that little piece of information to herself. In her mind's eye, she already knew the best locations for the shoots. But in order to maintain this facade, she had to look ignorant. Which, while it was something he expected, went totally against her grain.

"There you go, getting your feathers all ruffled again. And you shouldn't do that, honey. You know, with all that peanut butter ... things could get a little *sticky*," Mitch said, his blue eyes dancing with laughter. Then he reached out a hand and tucked a stray hair behind her ear. "Well, almighty map expert, where to?"

Giselle's gaze roamed over his golden hair. The billboard man was certainly more alluring than sin, but his prehistoric arrogance was beyond irritating. Where to, he wanted to know? How about off a steep cliff? Right offhand, she could think of several. In fact, she'd be happy to guide him to one herself. Instead, she leaned toward him and softly said, "Some advice, Mitch. Don't give up your day job. You'd never make it as a comedian."

Eyes like blue fire narrowed, his smile flattened to a straight line. Ha! Scored a dead ringer on that one, she thought with a sense of satisfaction.

Sliding on her sunglasses, she gave him what she hoped was her most innocent look. "Pull out onto this road right here, and follow it all the way down," she said sweetly, pointing a finger at the driveway. At his can-it look, she pretended to study the map.

Their first stop was a cove in which the water glistened calm and clear, almost translucent. A jagged cliff surrounded the half-circle that acted as a protective barrier from the wind and the waves. On one side, the brown volcanic rocks leading down to the grainy beach formed a natural staircase.

As in her childhood, Giselle skipped down the ledge with practiced ease. Reaching the beach, she wanted to strip off her clothing and dive into the cool depths of the water. She looked back at Mitch. Two camera bags slung over each shoulder hampered his progress as he picked his way down.

When he reached her, he commented, "What are you, part monkey?"

"I thought you knew, considering your generous breakfast of bananas this morning," she shot back, then turned to gaze out over the water. She couldn't stand it a second longer. It had been so long, and this had been one of her favorite spots in which to swim. She began tugging her top over her head.

Eyes wide, Mitch reached a hand out to stop her. "What are you doing?"

"Going for a swim, of course." Giselle shrugged off the hand that gripped her arm.

Very deliberately and carefully, he set down the camera bags. A look of exasperation written on his face, he loomed in front of her, his hands on his hips. "Legs, we're here to work, not play. That comes later, after we map out all the best locations this island has to offer. We have two days before the rest of the crew gets here. Even though this island is small, there's a lot of ground to cover."

Giselle pulled her shirt back down over her bathing-suit top. "Oh, yeah, I forgot."

"You forgot? Honey, if you think this is a vacation, then think again. You ought to know, modeling is hard work, especially under this blazing sun."

Oops, another slip, Giselle. She had to remember the part she was playing. But most importantly, she had to remember her goal—to win the bet. And right now, she was doing a lousy job at both.

Mitch turned away, unloaded several cameras and slung them over his shoulder. She walked up to him and tapped him on the back. "Sorry, Mitch. I guess I got carried away. The island, the beach, the water, it's all so beautiful, so tempting . . ." Her words faded as he straightened, striking her immobile with eyes that blazed with an emotion that had nothing to do with anger.

"Just like you, Legs. Tempting . . . and beautiful, *exactly* like you."

Deliberately, he set down the cameras and took a long look at her from her toes to the top of her head. "Let's see what we can do."

His hands released her hair from the ponytail she had put it in for convenience's sake. As for arranging the curls as he had done in the studio, the wind took care of that. The soft summer breeze tousled her dark strands, lifting them off the nape of her neck, and blowing them back, away from her face.

But he wasn't finished yet. Dear God, she discovered he wasn't anywhere close. With deliberate tenderness, he cupped her face, lowered his head and pressed a gentle kiss to each corner of her mouth. However, he didn't stop there. The tip of his tongue teased her lips, moistening them with his taste, before he parted them, delving inside. Harder and more insistent, Mitch deepened the kiss, taking her lips, possessing them, drinking from them, taking what she couldn't help but offer. And Giselle opened herself for more.

Blood sang through her body, hardening her nipples against his chest. She wanted more, so much more, than just his mouth on hers. She wanted his lips, his moist tongue everywhere, and all at once. Never before had she felt such intense desire. Surely, any minute now the refrain of "Love Is a Many Splendored Thing" sung by her happy hormones, would reach his ears. Her control was on the verge of slipping. And it was slipping fast, almost as fast as the racing beat of her heart, as fast as the multiplying demand of her hormones.

Right when she would have sunk to the sand, bringing him with her, he pulled back. He studied her kiss-swollen lips, down to the erect nipples that peaked against her cotton top.

"Okay, Legs, keep that look, except kneel down in the sand." Mitch pushed her down. "Good, now spread those long, luscious legs of yours. That's it. Now hold it."

He whipped around and snatched up one of his cameras. Before Giselle knew what had hit her, there he was, clicking off one picture after another, as if nothing had happened. Apparently, to him, nothing had. But for her, the world had stopped for that one precious moment, her body had come to life, her lost and presumed-missing hormones had been found, alive and *very* well.

However, it didn't take long for the anger to bubble to the surface along with those blasted hiccups. She surged to her feet.

"That's it! Yes. Great! Now move around. Wonderful." Mitch lowered the camera and frowned. "Wait a minute, Legs. You're getting a little too close to the lens."

Hiccup. "You . . . kissed," *hiccup*, ". . . just to get me—" She stopped. *Hiccup.*

"Spit it out, honey."

Giselle balled up one fist and punched him in the arm. "How dare you!" She pulled back throbbing knuckles.

Seemingly unaffected, Mitch grinned at her. "It worked, didn't it? And I'd be willing to bet you even enjoyed it."

Hiccup. "I'm not a plaything, Mr. Sullivan. I don't work that way."

Dark blue eyes turned to icy blue chips of fury. "You're not working, *period*, as far as I can tell. Now grab a bite of your damned peanut butter and let's get back to work."

And work her he did, for the rest of the day, from one beach to the next until they'd made their way all around the island. Exhausted and weary, Giselle couldn't manage to smile once more or wet and pout her lips one more time.

"Okay, next shot. Over here, Legs." Mitch motioned her to the pile of stones. "Now, drape your-

self over them. Good, but bend back a little farther
. . . farther.''

"Time!" Giselle moaned and made the familiar
T-gesture with her hands since a white flag conceding
surrender was nowhere to be found. "I can't go on.
For heaven's sake, Mitch, I'm not a contortionist."
She straightened and flexed her back muscles. "Can't
we call it a day?"

Mitch glanced at the waning light of the sunset.
"Okay, Legs, you win. And I must admit, you've been
a real sport. I've never gotten so much work out of
a model before. Usually they're so temperamental."

Giselle spun around and jumped in the Jeep, mut-
tering to herself. Temperamental, huh? By damn, she
could show him temperamental about now. If she
had known she could get away with it, she would have
bitched all day, not only to aggravate him but to
play the part more accurately. Instead, she'd worked
herself to utter exhaustion. A good sport, was she?
Well, she ought to show him. Yeah, that's what she
ought to do. But, heaven help her, she didn't have
the energy.

When he joined her in the Jeep, she couldn't mus-
ter the energy to even acknowledge him. Not that
she would have anyway. And as curved and bumpy
as the road was on the way to the house, Giselle could
barely manage to keep her eyes open.

The Jeep came to a jerky stop, snatching her back
from the verge of slumber. Not bothering to help
unload the equipment, or to wait for Mitch, Giselle
plodded up the stairs to the porch, with two thoughts
in mind: a shower, then bed.

But those thoughts vanished as Mitch's deep voice
stopped her in her tracks. "Legs?"

She turned and looked at him. He stood at the
bottom of the steps, leaning toward her, one foot on

the ground, the other two steps up. It was almost as if, in some small way, he wanted to reach out to her. As angry as she was at him, she couldn't deny the tiny urge that told her to go to him, and wrap herself up in his arms. Somehow, she resisted by gripping the doorknob.

"Look, the kiss this morning. It wasn't just to get the look I wanted. I don't work that way either. I kissed you," he paused and took a deep breath, "because I wanted to."

Chapter Seven

Moonlight illuminated the sandy beach in ghostly bands like ribbons. The celestial glow rippled off the gently lapping waves. The air was calm, almost eerily so, as if the winds waited, like Giselle herself, with anticipation for the next storm, the next rising tide, the next kiss . . .

I kissed you because I wanted to . . .

Mitch's words played through her mind over and over, sparking a ray of hope, igniting a flame of desire. Exhausted as she had been from the long day's work, Giselle found herself restless and unable to sleep. After counting dozens of sheep, she finally gave up the fight. Each sheep bore a dangerous resemblance to Mitch, the white coat replaced with a tiny white towel, a silky mane of golden hair and eyes a vibrant blue.

The beach and the soothing sounds of the Gulf beckoned to her. A refreshing dip in the warm waters off the Florida Keys was exactly what she needed.

Maybe that would clear her mind, cool the aching want that his softly spoken words had invoked, water down her rapidly charging hormones.

Donning a leopard-print bikini and a lace cover-up, Giselle slipped out the patio door and down the wooden steps that led to the beach. She dropped her towel and shrugged off the lace. For a few blessed moments, she faced the water, reveling in the soft summer breeze and the ethereal tropical beauty that surrounded her. The wind caressed her skin with breathless fingers, gently lifting her hair, cooling her neck, sending shivers down her spine.

Paradise. This was as close as it came. No wonder her father had named the island after the only word to encompass its natural state.

As she had longed to do all day, Giselle ran toward the water's edge, carefree and so much like the little girl who had once played and romped along this very same beach.

Right as her foot hit the water, a bear-hug tackle knocked her to the sand. A terrified scream tore from her throat, and using every self-defense move she knew, she began to struggle.

"Calm down, Legs. It's only me," Mitch said, carefully avoiding the clenched fists she sent his way.

She stopped her sorry imitation of Chuck Norris. "Mitch?"

"Who did you expect?" He rolled her beneath him, his thighs pinning her to the sand. "The Skipper? Or Gilligan?" His face was bathed in shadow, but his body was achingly clear to her—every muscle, every hard curve, every inch of warmth.

Tepid salt water seeped under her as a wave slid to the shore. Her nerve-shattering shock gone, anger infused her next words. "Why in the hell did you do that?"

"Do what?" Even though she couldn't see his face, his voice was full of teasing and smiles. In fact, she was surprised his perfectly white teeth didn't glow in the dark.

"Tackle me, that's what. I was going for a swim, not playing wide receiver for the Paradise Packers."

He shifted his weight slightly, and it seemed Giselle's body was now even closer to his. "Against the rules, Legs."

"What are you talking about? And let me up. You're squashing me." She squirmed beneath his pressing weight, but when she felt the undeniable hardness press against the tiny triangle of her bikini, she stilled.

"Good girl," he whispered in what sounded like a strained voice. With an elbow propped on each side of her head, Mitch raised himself partially off her. "Rule number one, no swimming by yourself, especially at night. And rule number two—"

"Come on. What is this? The Marines? Oh, let me guess. You must be Sergeant Carter, or is that Gomer Pyle?"

"Very funny."

"Mitch, we're not working now. This is my time."

"And you're my model, so you're *my* responsibility."

Giselle groaned. The last thing she needed was for him to see her as merely a responsibility. A burden. How many times had she heard her father speak these very same words? Too many to count.

"I'm just doing what's best for you, Legs."

With the exception of the nickname, she could have sworn dear old Dad was talking to her.

"Rule number two, no swimming, period—"

"But—"

"At least not in salt water. I know it's early in the

season, but the last thing we need is for you to mar
that lovely skin with a jellyfish sting.''

The water lapped at her hair, and Mitch fingered
a dark swirling curl that floated in it. ''According
to the map, there's a freshwater lagoon somewhere
inland. Until we finish the shoot, I have to insist that
you swim only there. For your own protection, and
for my peace of mind.''

''This shoot means a lot to you, doesn't it?'' she
asked, nibbling at her lower lip.

''It could be the turning point in my career.''

A twinge of guilt stabbed at Giselle. Mitch was
counting on this layout to boost his career, and here
she was messing it all up for him. She should tell him
the truth now, while there was still time left to get
another model. A real one.

''Mitch—'' she began, but then sputtered as a wave
crashed over them, soaking them both. ''Look,'' she
said, pushing her flattened palms against his chest,
''I'd love to stay here and reenact the scene in *From
Here to Eternity,* but would you mind getting off me
before another wave rolls in?''

Another wave covered them. Mitch shook the water
from his hair. ''Too late, Legs. I think this is the part
where I'm supposed to kiss you.''

She started to protest, but her words were lost as
his warm, wet lips captured hers in a caress that was
moonlight and velvet combined.

Thinking nothing, yet feeling everything with wondrous intensity, Giselle gave herself to his kiss. That is,
until the next wave rolled over them and the burning
sting of salt water traveled up her nose.

As she began to choke, he released his delicious
possession of her mouth. ''I . . . I think the tide must
be rising.''

Again, she couldn't make out the features on his

face, but she knew he was smiling. "Honey, that isn't the only thing that's rising." And to prove his point, he pressed his hips against hers. Threads of heat coiled through her, only to be doused as another wave washed over them. Then another.

"I think you may be right," Mitch admitted. He jumped to his feet and extended a hand. Cautiously, she placed her hand in his and he lifted her to her feet.

Giselle wasn't sure whether she felt relief or disappointment when he pulled her farther up the bank, spread out her towel and sat down. "Let's talk, Legs." He patted the space next to him.

"What? More rules?" She crossed her arms over her bare midriff and put herself immediately on the defensive. After all, she wasn't used to taking orders, she was used to giving them. With the exception of her father. But what weighed on her mind more than anything was, once again Mitch had kissed her, sending her common sense scrambling, and her hormones off the scale. While he didn't seem the least bit affected by it, she felt like a yo-yo. She only wished when he pulled her into the warmth of his hand, he would keep her there, instead of flinging her back out again.

Bright moonlight reflected off the white sand. Now his features were strikingly clear in the soft light. Thick, wet hair was pushed back off his forehead. Beads of water still trickled down his face. The cutoff shorts he wore were faded and dangerously thin in the most strategic places. His chest was temptingly bare, his six-pack belly rippled with rock-hard muscles. Even in the midnight sky, his smile glowed, his dimples deep slits at the sides of his mouth.

With an amazing speed Giselle still hadn't come to expect, Mitch grabbed her hand and pulled her down to the spot beside him. "No more rules. Right now, just friendly talk. Tell me about yourself, Giselle. Tell me about this fascinating, gorgeous, long-legged creature, with a definite fetish for peanut butter."

"I . . . I . . ." She shifted on the sand and threaded a trembling hand through her tangled hair. "What do you want to know?"

"Where are you from?"

Hormone heaven.

"How did you get into modeling?"

Lord, you wouldn't believe me if I told you.

"You know, things like that."

Think fast, Giselle.

Better yet, here's the opportune moment to tell him the truth.

But what about dear old Dad? How am I going to explain this whole situation to him? Especially about the money. That blasted money Anita would be demanding the moment Giselle failed.

"Well, let's see. I was born and raised in Houston, the only child of a very loving mother and an overbearing father, who wished I had been born on Mars."

"What? Mars?"

"You know, *Men Are from Mars, Women Are from Venus?*"

His look of confusion grew.

"Forget it. As for modeling, I kind of . . . fell into it just recently." *Nothing like a smidgen of truth.* She mocked her effort to avoid the guilt of outright lying. Besides, if her nose grew any more, she'd put Pinocchio and every circus elephant on earth out of business.

Mitch sat with legs bent, his arms resting on his knees, his eyes trained on her every move. "What else, Giselle? Who are you, really? What do you want out of life?"

What did she want out of life? Right at the moment, she wanted to win the blasted bet and get off the island before she totally lost her mind, and her heart. *And* made a complete fool of herself.

"Legs?" Mitch reached out one long finger and trailed it up her bare thigh.

"I guess I never really thought about it." She laughed nervously.

"You mean, you haven't made it a goal to earn twenty thousand a day as a model?" He sounded cynical.

"I'd like to make enough to support myself, have some independence, cut those blasted apron strings, that's for sure, but—"

"Maybe twenty thousand a day isn't enough to keep you in silk underwear and a nice roomy Mercedes," Mitch scoffed.

"Excuse me?"

"Perhaps thirty thousand is more up your alley. I haven't met a model yet who doesn't have high aspirations." The muscles in his jaw bunched as he worked it back and forth in a grinding motion.

"How nice. Another sexist remark. Give me a break, Mitch. I've told you, I'm not like most models. Money isn't that important to me. I'd rather have happiness. Besides, I've seen firsthand that money doesn't always insure it." Giselle cupped a handful of sand and sifted it from one hand to the next. "What about you, Mitch? And what about that billboard?"

"I'd rather forget about that damned billboard. That's not my game, I've seen my sister go through one man after another she met from singles' ads. And every time, she's ended up with a broken heart, not to mention, a broken pocketbook. No, that's not for me. I prefer to find my own women, when and where I want them."

To Giselle it seemed the sand had turned into murky, deadly quicksand into which she was sinking deeper and deeper with every word he spoke. The situation looked bleak, to say the least. Maybe there was some other way she could cough up the five thousand. She feared this was one bet she couldn't win.

"Are you," she cleared her throat, "are you seeing anyone special right now?"

Relief spilled through her as Mitch shook his head. "No. I got burned when I became involved with a model I worked with. She was the type who wanted forty thousand a day—and would do anything to get it." A smile tinged with bitterness curved the corners of his mouth. "So that's another rule of mine. No more models."

Giselle swallowed hard, and the relief vanished. Not only did the situation look bleak, it was downright dead in the water. Maybe Anita would take the winnings on installments.

No more models? That was what he had said, emphatically. His words sank in and finally registered in her racing brain. Anger simmered just below the surface as she turned to him. "No models? Then what exactly am I? And why do you keep kissing me if I'm against your so-called rules?"

Long moments passed before he looked at her and answered in a low, husky voice that vibrated all the way to her innermost core, "I don't know, Legs. I wish to God I did, so I could stop. You're so different from any other model I've worked with—"

"That's because I'm not—"

Mitch placed a finger over her lips. "Shhh, I know. You're not like most models. You don't have to keep reminding me because I know . . ." In a whisper of a touch, the tip of his nail traced her lips. "I've known that from the very beginning. That's why this is so hard for me. I want you, yet I can't, or maybe I should say, I shouldn't." His finger left her lips and trailed over her face, then dipped to the valley between her breasts. "Just from what I've learned, I know you wouldn't be interested in a quick fling. But, honey, that's all I can offer you."

His touch sent her pulse racing and a hot flush spread all the way to her toes. She closed her eyes. A quick fling? He was right. It wasn't her style. But, heaven help her, she wanted him. She had from the start. Besides, a voice inside her head taunted, a quick fling was all she needed to win the bet.

Unaware that his breath had all but stopped, Mitch waited. Blood hammered through him, wrenching at his self-control. All he wanted to do at that moment was take the tiny strips of cloth from her body and look at her bathed in moonlight—touch her, taste her, sheathe himself in her until there was nothing but her passionate heat wrapped around him. He had laid it all out for her, had been totally honest. He could give her his body, but his heart wouldn't be part of the deal. It couldn't be.

His finger continued to trace lazy circles over her chest, inching toward her lovely breasts barely concealed by the skimpy bikini top, while he waited for some sign from her. He skimmed her smooth, silky skin one more time and felt desire roll through him like thunder echoing through a thick, island jungle.

His gaze lifted to her face. Her lips were full and wet and parted, their pouting curves a silent invitation to a man's hungry mouth. And Mitch was starving. He leaned toward her and slowly lowered his head, waiting for her to protest or, hopefully, draw him near.

She smelled of moonlight, tropical flowers and a

distant Gulf storm. A sound like a cascading sigh escaped her sweet lips, and Mitch could no longer resist. Once, twice, then again and again, he brushed his mouth against hers, tasting her with the tip of his tongue, taking tiny sips of her until her lips parted helplessly—hungrily.

Giselle lifted a hand to his cheek. The gentle touch of her fingers made him shudder as though he'd been brushed by lightning. That one jagged streak soon turned into a raging storm.

"Tell me, honey," he murmured against her lips. "Tell me what you want."

"I want . . . just kiss me, Mitch. Hold me . . . love me." Her dark green eyes gleamed like the sea touched by moonlight.

"But you know it can only be for here . . . now," he said so softly his words were little more than a regretful sigh.

"I know . . . Touch me, please. I burn where you touch me. So burn me, right here, right now. I *need* you to *really* . . . touch me," she whispered, then pulled him toward her, lacing her fingers through his hair.

Mitch eased her down onto her back. Her dark hair scattered in an untamed cloud against the white sand. Her luscious body glowed with the blush of ripened fruit; her proud breasts thrust tightly against the thin nylon of her top, her nipples little pebbles, hard and erect.

The sight of her sent hot claws of desire raking through him; their razor-sharp points sinking into him until they urged him on, driving him to madness. Mitch searched for some sense of control, but found none. Her sweet soft mouth beckoned to him, her hardened nipples called out for his lips, his touch.

The waves now crashed to the shore as the tide

rose. The calm wind that had once caressed the island like a lover's touch, now whipped about them wildly. As wildly as the blood flowing through him, as turbulent as the desire that escalated into a demanding need. But Mitch hardly noticed that the changing climate matched his own passionate desperation as he untied the strings to Giselle's top.

Her breasts stood full and firm, tipped with tight pink crowns. With reverent hands, he took the weight of her in his palms, his thumbs flicking her nipples into full pink buds.

Giselle arched into his caress and wrapped her arms around him. Her touch sent pinpoints of fire through him like thousands of exploding lights. He claimed her lips once again, and her mouth blossomed under his much as fragrant flowers part their petals to the sun.

Wanting to taste her everywhere and all at once, he blazed a trail down the curve of her neck, stopping to lick and press openmouthed kisses before he lowered his lips to the valley between her breasts. With slow deliberation, he bestowed gentle kisses that traced the rich curves of a breast, in ever smaller circles, until he reached its thrusting ready center. Over and over, he curled his tongue around the pink buds and drew them into his mouth, suckling, drawing her to him, until she arched like a taut bow and scored her nails down his back, crying out his name.

Being torn between what he wanted and what he knew he shouldn't have made him wild. After all, she was his model. And he was breaking his own rules. Right now, in the heat of passion, she would consent to a brief fling, but Mitch knew things would change. It happened every time. Women, he found, always wanted commitment. And that was something he wasn't willing to give.

But how could he back down now? He wanted her like no other. Exquisite pleasure combined with torment to gnaw at his gut as desire knifed through him, reminding him what he should not have.

Abruptly, he pulled back. "Giselle, I—"

She sat up, a look of bewilderment on her lovely face. "Mitch, is something wrong?"

Raking a stiff hand through his hair, he muttered, "Yes . . . no. I'd better go back to the bungalow before I do something I'll regret later."

And without another word, he sprang to his feet and ran to the house as if demons were chasing him, leaving Giselle with an icy feeling in her heart that soon melted in the heat of anger. Angry with herself for being so willing in his arms, and positively furious with Mitch for taking what she offered and then throwing it back in her face. Hormones that just a few moments ago were rejoicing like a heavenly choir, now rolled over and played dead. Her heart instantly became a dull, leaden weight in her chest. A weight so heavy, she was surprised it was still beating.

Embarrassment and humiliation marked her every step, but somehow Giselle managed to make it back to her room. *God, how can I ever face him in the morning?* She had practically begged him to make love to her. What had she been thinking? That was the problem. She hadn't been thinking at all. Desire and passion and her only-the-lonely hormones had taken over her common sense. And look where it had gotten her.

A shower didn't help dispel the red-hot want that still throbbed through her or the burning embarrassment. And it seemed sleep wouldn't give her the release she craved, either. For even in her restless slumber, she felt his touch, tasted his lips, craved his heated possession. And in her dreams, he claimed her, sent her to the heavens and back. In her dreams, she wasn't just a quick fling. No, far from it. In her dreams, she was Mitch's sweet Texas lady. The one that he wanted . . . the one that he loved.

Chapter Eight

"Ahoy, there," a booming voice squawked over the shortwave. "Is anybody there? Come in, come in . . . wherever you are. Over."

Zipping his blue-jean shorts the rest of the way up, Mitch rushed into the study, grabbed the handheld mike and pressed the button. "This is Paradise Key. Come in. Over."

"Well, hello there, little buddy. How goes it in Paradise?" came the familiar drawl.

Wearily, Mitch rubbed his eyes. Last night had been a sleepless one, and the very last thing he needed this morning was to talk to Curtis.

"Hello? Are you there? Over."

Mitch sighed then slid into the rolling chair. "Curtis, how did you get this shortwave number? Over."

"Like I've told you before, partner, I've got connections in high places. So tell me, master, has the genie popped out of the bottle yet? Over."

"Give it a break, Rockhead. Over."

"No luck, huh? Must be losing your touch, Midas man. Over."

He was losing something, all right. Probably his mind. Last night, he had held Giselle in his arms and could have made love to her right there under the stars, but he'd backed out. Yep, he had definitely lost his mind, because his body was still demanding answers. One thing was certain, he was in no mood to talk, least of all to Curtis.

Mitch pressed the button. "Is there a purpose for this call, or did you just want to bug me? Over."

"Me? Bug you? Not on your life. Actually, I wasn't too sure if you've kept up with the news, but, little buddy, you may be doing an imitation of Gilligan sooner than you think. Over."

Mitch's frustration level reached its peak. "Curtis, get to it," he barked into the mike. "What in the hell are you talking about? Over."

"Well, I wouldn't exactly say it's definite, but a storm is abrewing out in them there waters. Over."

"A storm? What kind of storm? Over." A flash of alarm sizzled down Mitch's spine.

"Now, now, don't get all excited. Hurricane Brutus may not even hit the Keys, but then again, you may want to alert the Skipper and Mary Ann. Over."

Mitch's alarm solidified into one big pit of dread in the depth of his stomach. "Do you have the coordinates? Over."

As Curtis called out the longitude and latitude, Mitch pinpointed the location of the eye of the storm on the map that hung on the wall. A little sigh of relief spread through him. It was to the southeast of Paradise Key, headed due west. If it stayed on its present course, they should have no problem. But considering the ever-changing warm Gulf waters, the hurricane could turn in any direction, at any time.

"Thanks for the info, Curtis. For once, you were a big help. Over."

"Okay, little buddy. But remember, this might be your last chance to go for it. Don't pull a Professor. He never would put the make on Ginger. Big mistake, if you ask me. So just do it! Over and out, aloha, so long, farewell, and all that kind of stuff."

Pushing back from the radio, Mitch went to the desk and rummaged in the drawers. There had to be emergency numbers for the Coast Guard somewhere.

"What in the hell do you think you're doing?" Giselle demanded from the doorway.

His hand stopped in midair. Before glancing up, Mitch braced himself for the sight of her. Then he turned his head and drank in every sweet precious bit of Giselle, from her beautiful emerald eyes down over the white crop-top with matching drawstring shorts to those tempting never-ending legs that haunted his dreams.

Mentally, he gave himself a shake and opened the next drawer. "I'm looking for something."

Giselle marched over to him and grabbed his hand. "That's obvious. I thought we already had a discussion about snooping."

Even when she was angry, her touch sent electric shock waves up his arm, and they immediately spiraled down to his groin. He resisted the urge to yank her down onto his lap and kiss her until she had no breath left to protest.

Instead he sighed. "Listen, Legs, I'm just trying to find a shortwave number. We may have a little trouble headed our way."

Frowning, she released his hand and perched herself on the edge of the desk. "What kind of trouble?"

Her long, dangling legs hypnotized him, once again stirring up memories of last night and what had almost happened between them. Finally, he found his reply, not to mention, his brain, which seemed to have just gone south . . . to man's land. "Uh, a hurricane by the name of Brutus."

Giselle tilted her head back and closed her eyes. Even though Anita had mentioned it, the tropical depression had totally slipped her mind. "Where is it?"

Mitch's eyes narrowed. "You don't seem too surprised."

"I . . . er, well, I heard something about a depression brewing before we left Houston."

"Oh, I see." He stepped closer to her and crossed his arms. "You just didn't see the need to tell me about it."

Leftover irritation from his rejection last night, along with a miserable night of tossing and turning, had her stewing. His nearness, his temptingly bare chest and the top button of his shorts, which he'd left undone, did nothing to improve her mood, either. Regardless of what had happened, she was still drawn to him like a bee is to honey. However, his highhanded attitude was too much for her to stomach just now.

Giselle stood and looked him in the eye. "Don't you have a TV or a radio at home? I'm your model, Mr. Sullivan, not your personal weather forecaster. Do I look like Willard Scott to you?"

She whirled and walked to the window that overlooked the calm, crystal aquamarine water. Early morning sunshine spilled onto the sand below, making it glint like stardust. "Besides, it doesn't look like a hurricane's on the way to me. It's calm and beautiful, even serene. It's paradise."

"Yeah, the calm before the storm," he muttered.

Giselle glanced at him. "Maybe. Then again," she studied the hurricane map that had a red bead where Mitch had already tracked the storm, "it looks as if it may pass to the south."

She flipped open the Rolodex that sat on the desk. "If you're looking for numbers, it seems to me the logical place to find them is in here." She turned and walked to the door, then called over her shoulder, "Breakfast is in five minutes."

Giselle slipped into the kitchen and leaned against the counter. Lord, that was a close one.

Hiccup.

If Mitch had searched any further, he might have come across something to reveal her true identity. He couldn't find out, not just yet.

Hiccup.

And the last thing she needed was for that stupid Brutus to pounce on the island. If she could stand it, she wanted a few more days alone with Mitch. As it was, the sight of his bare chest this morning had almost sent her into a whirlwind of her own—rightly named Hurricane Hormone.

Although, after last night, Giselle wasn't so sure she could continue with this charade. It had now become more than just winning a bet or avoiding her father's wrath. Unfortunately, her heart had gotten involved in the whole mess.

Pushing away from the counter, she opened a cabinet and took out the jumbo jar of peanut butter. She swirled a finger in its rich creaminess and popped it into her mouth. Satisfied the habit was under control, she absently scrambled a half-dozen eggs mixed with onions, bell peppers and cheese to go with some English muffins she had toasted. She had just placed a bowl of mixed fruit on the table when Mitch walked in, fully clothed.

"What is all this?" he asked, genuine surprise written on his face.

"This," she gave him the barest of looks, "is a proper breakfast. Tomorrow it's your turn. That is, *if* we're still here."

Mitch pulled out a chair, sat down and reached

for a cup of coffee. "I called the Coast Guard, and right now, there's no mandatory evacuation."

From a large white decanter, Giselle poured the rich java into his cup and then her own. "Mitch, don't you think if we were in any danger, Mr. Grant would see to our safety?"

A sheepish look flooded his face. "You're right. Maybe I'm overreacting. But you," his deep blue eyes assessed her thoroughly, "don't seem a bit upset. I figured you'd be hiccuping all over the place."

Giselle squashed down the urge to give him a swift kick under the table. "Why? Because I'm a woman? Hate to disappoint you, Mitch, but I've been there, done that," she quipped.

"Done what?" Mitch loaded his plate with the Southwestern-style egg mixture and two muffins.

"Hurricanes. Living on the coast all my life, I've been through my share."

He gave her an incredulous look. "And you're not afraid of them?"

"I have a healthy respect for Mother Nature. But being afraid is something entirely different." At the moment, the only thing she feared was losing her heart to this man who had sapphire jewels for eyes and dimples to die for. Granted, she wanted him, but somehow she had to maintain some distance emotionally. Otherwise, last night wouldn't be the only sleepless night she would have. No, she thought, stealing a peek at him, if her heart and those pesky hormones had any say in the matter, it would be the first of many.

One hour later, they rumbled down the island's only road.

"Take a left . . . right here." Giselle pointed to the little dirt track that was a break in the thick vegetation.

Mitch eyed the opening, barely big enough to accommodate the Jeep. "Are you sure?"

"Me-navigator, you-driver. Remember?"

He grunted. "I thought the saying went something like, me-Tarzan, you-Jane."

"If that were true, Mr. King of the Jungle, and you had put in your time on the vine, you'd know that this is the correct turn."

Mitch looked as if he had some smart comment to add, but instead, he grunted again and carefully turned the Jeep onto the path, shifting down as they climbed steadily into the hills. The rough road bounced them about on their seats, and Giselle held on to the roll bar to keep from ending up in Mitch's lap.

The towering mangrove and palm jungle provided a natural canopy over their heads. Periodically shafts of sunlight peeped through. The leaves and branches of various flowering trees occasionally snagged them, like hungry fingers wanting to snatch them back from the paradise Giselle knew lay just ahead.

The higher they climbed, the cooler the breeze, the denser the lush vegetation, until they had no alternative but to stop the Jeep.

"Looks like it's on foot from here," Mitch commented as he swung out of the driver's seat.

"It isn't much farther." Giselle stopped when he looked at her curiously. "Uh, according to the map, I mean."

"Uh-huh. Well, bring it with you just in case we get lost," he ordered, unloading the camera equipment and slinging the bags over his shoulders.

Giselle gathered some towels, snacks and a canteen

full of water into one mesh bag, then started up the tiny path that was barely a path at all.

"Wait, Legs." Mitch reached out a restraining hand. "The map."

"Oh . . . yeah, the map, I almost forgot." She reached into the Jeep and took it out. Although she knew the trail by heart, she pretended to study it. "Yep, I was right. This is the way."

After several minutes of steady walking through twists and turns, up and down a trail barely six inches wide, and numerous disagreements later about which way was the right way, Mitch and Giselle finally came to a halt.

"Shhh, listen," she whispered.

The hush of the deep jungle magnified the clear echo of water trickling downward. She grabbed his hand and hurried around the next bend into a small clearing.

Soft, green moss covered the ground surrounding the natural ledge of flat rocks that encompassed a gentle, swirling, crystal-clear lagoon. A jagged hill rose on one side, where a beautiful waterfall spilled and splashed, emptying its cool spring-fed water into the stillness of the lagoon. Bougainvilleas and huge red hibiscus trees bloomed in vibrant color all around the special oasis.

"Paradise," Mitch murmured as he gazed at his surroundings. "Absolute paradise."

"Yes, this is as close as it comes," Giselle agreed, setting down the towels, her voice hushed. Her eyes absorbed every inch of her favorite private hideaway. Not many people had seen this spot on the island. In her teens, Giselle had discovered it while exploring on her own. And though it was drawn on the map, she always considered this special place to be her very own.

Mitch set down the camera bags and walked around the small lagoon, his eyes measuring, assessing. "Exquisite. This is perfect."

Giselle smiled as she watched him. This place had had the same effect on her the first time she had seen it. And each time, its beauty increased, along with her appreciation for the almost sacred wonder it made her feel.

Enthusiasm radiated from eyes whose color matched that of the depths of the lagoon as he said, "The whole island is wonderful for the layout, but this . . . this place is perfect—for the entire issue."

He tore into the camera bags. "We'll start with shots along the outside, and then I want you to get in the water, on the ledges, under the waterfall."

Giselle stripped off her shorts and top, down to one of the bikinis that Grant's had provided. Encrusted with sparkling rhinestones, the white Brazilian-cut suit left almost nothing to the imagination. She fought the urge to cover herself with her hands, hoping to reveal a little less.

But even as she thought to do so, Mitch whispered, his voice husky and deep, "Leave it, Legs. You look perfect." He plucked a giant red bloom and tucked it behind her ear. "You look like an island princess. No wonder Warren picked you for this layout."

And damn him for doing so, Mitch thought. For now, Giselle was off limits. If he had met her in another time, another place, there would be no rules. Nothing would stop him from taking her, loving her. As it was, the strain of keeping his hands off her bore down on him, unmercifully. And he wasn't sure how much longer he could resist. Especially as she looked now.

Trying to get his wants and desires under control, Mitch shook himself and slipped into the business role he had to play. A role he *must* play, whether he liked it or not. "Okay, Legs, let's start over here. Now lie down on the rock and smile for me, honey." He swallowed hard, his voice strangely hoarse to his own ears. "Think sensual, baby. Think want . . . desire . . . seduction."

Click . . . click.

"Yes, that's it. Now wet your lips and arch your back."

And for the next few hours, Giselle posed and smiled and wet her lips until Mitch thought he would explode from the relentless desire eating away at him. The overwhelming ache refused to leave him alone, no matter how many times he reminded himself that Giselle was his model and he was there to work. *Just work.*

Click . . . click, click, click.

Grace and beauty combined with ease and poise. This was Giselle Green. But more than that drew Mitch to her—the way she laughed, her sharp intelligence, even her unusual quirks made him want her.

She's off limits, Sullivan, the irritating voice reminded him again.

But that echoing annoying voice disappeared when, on the last shoot, Giselle emerged from a small cave hidden behind the waterfall. Crowning nipples peaked under the wet, almost transparent white top. The tiny bikini bottom revealed her every curve. Her dark, sleek hair hung like satin between her shoulder blades.

Mitch snapped the zoom lens into place and focused on just her face. Pure pleasure glowed from her every feature as she stood on the ledge beneath the cool, gentle waterfall. Water glided over her like sensuous hands sliding over her skin, touching every part of her in exactly the way Mitch wanted to touch her. And touch her he would. He had to. Rules be damned. He couldn't stand it anymore.

He eased his camera to the ground, whipped off his shorts, and dove into the cool, clear water. But even the coolness of the water did nothing to ease the heat that pumped almost painfully through his body. No, nothing would cool his desire. Only one person could do that. His sweet Texas lady.

No longer posing or modeling, Giselle lifted her face to the cascading water. Pure enjoyment overrode any other thought. Never before had the cool water felt like a lover's caress. Never before had her skin felt so heated even in the midst of the coolness.

She pushed back the wet hair from her face and looked around for Mitch, but saw no one. The hand that reached up to clamp around her foot sent her heart to pounding.

"You scared me—" The words caught in her throat as she looked down into the clear depths of the lagoon and saw that Mitch wore nothing. Anita was right. He did have a great set of apple-cheeked buns.

"Come, my little mermaid. Come swim with me," he said in that all-too-familiar deep, husky voice that melted her resolve.

With one jerk of his hand, Giselle lost her balance and flew over his head, landing in the water with a splash. She came up sputtering, "Why . . . why did you do that?"

Slowly, he swam to her, and Giselle could almost hear the strains to the theme from *Jaws.* His slow swim turned to a purposeful walk when he could stand on the sandy bottom. His steady stare felt like a searing blast of heat, burning her skin even as the cool water swirled around her. She felt exposed, almost naked, as if she didn't have the tiny bikini on at all.

"I did *that,* because I wanted to do *this,*" he whispered before two muscular arms reached for her. He clasped her face between his large hands and kissed her gently, coaxing her lips apart, sipping at the droplets that trickled down her face.

Feeling everything, and all at once, Giselle gave herself to his kiss, losing herself in his taste. A caressing warmth that was the sunrise and feel of satin combined spread through her, and she shuddered.

"You're cold," he almost groaned. "I don't want you to be cold, Legs. I want you to be fire and silk under my fingers. I want you to burn where I touch you." His next words were a breathless flame against her lips. "And I intend to touch every last sweet inch of you."

He lifted her with hands that were both gentle and powerful, and placed her on the ledge. Pulling himself out of the water, Mitch swept her up into his arms once again, and walked to the spot where they had left the equipment and towels. He gently lowered her to the soft grass that created a heavenly, natural bed. With tender hands, he picked up a towel and rubbed its velvety softness over her, drying the water from her skin. And, helplessly, she found herself leaning toward him, seeking his touch, a whisper of a caress that ended almost before it began.

Through lowered lids, Giselle watched him. All male, proudly naked. Definitely anything but cardboard and glue.

His warm hands replaced the stroke of the towel. A luxuriant heat rippled through her, and her body arched in an automatic response. With slow, achingly deliberate movements, Mitch untied the bikini top and peeled down the skimpy bottom. All at once, her body became a wild, pulsating core of pure flame, burning higher and higher with a knowing hunger. A hunger that demanded to be fulfilled. A hunger that reminded her of how starved she was for this man.

"All warm now?" he murmured.

"Mmmm, more like hot," she gasped as his hands brushed her breasts in tormenting circles until her nipples pouted erect and hard, flushed with a begging heat.

"Hmmm, it's gonna get hotter." He gave her a sexy dimpled grin, then laughed. His laughter was as sensual as the wildfire that burned inside of her.

His tongue curled around one pink bud and then the other, drawing them into his mouth, spreading the uncontrollable blaze, sending it spiraling downward.

As delicately as a sigh, Mitch fingered her, teasing the hidden pearl of her want until ecstasy cascaded through her, spilling a silky heat over his hand. He delved a long finger deeply into her, retreated with aching slowness, drawing her essence with him, letting it drip between his fingers.

"Look, Legs. Look how wet you are, how you weep for me."

A bolt of shimmering lightning snapped through her and almost sent her over the edge again, with just his whispered words.

He slid his finger into her again and again, spreading the scent of her moisture until it clung to both of them like honeyed nectar to a blooming flower.

Giselle reached down and wrapped her hand around his pulsating manhood that stood hard, hot and erect. A deep, almost inaudible groan hissed between his clenched teeth. "Honey, I've got to have you." His entire body trembled beneath her touc'

"Damn the rules, I want you so much, it's like dying not to be inside you."

"Then have me . . ." she whispered into his mouth. "Take me. Now."

Softly, she parted for him, taking him even as she gave herself to him. Relentlessly, he drove into her, rocking against her, fitting himself deeply to her, then deeper, sweeter still.

With every probing circling penetration, Mitch whispered to her, praising her, coaxing her, loving her. His lingering kisses savored her, heightening her fire until she burned, sweetly—wildly. As wildly as the native flowers growing in the midst of paradise.

And to paradise she flew as a sunburst of fiery pleasure blazed and exploded deep within her. A few seconds later, Mitch followed her there. To paradise . . . where reality melted into oblivion . . . pleasure . . . ecstasy. Where it became one perfect whole. Where it became . . . love.

Chapter Nine

"What in the hell do you mean you're not coming?" Mitch barked into the mike.

"Sorry, boss. Like I said, insurance won't cover the crew and the rest of the equipment because of that hurricane down there. Over," came the static-filled response.

Mitch raked a stiff hand through his hair. "That hurricane is miles from here. Over."

"It isn't now. In fact, if I were you, I'd be hightailing it back to Miami, or better yet, farther north. Over."

A defeated sigh escaped his lips and Mitch closed his eyes. The job of his life seemed to be doomed before it had even begun. But more than that, he'd been so involved with Giselle, making love to her countless times at the lagoon and back at the bungalow since yesterday afternoon, that he'd completely forgotten about Brutus. In fact, the only storm that had been on his mind was the whirlwind of passion that drove him relentlessly to seek her time and time again. Delving deeper, yet not deep enough. Struggling to get closer, yet never close enough. Sating his hunger for her, yet still starved for her touch, her warmth . . .

He gave himself a mental shake and pried his thoughts away from his long-legged beauty and back to the crisis at hand. "Do you have the latest coordinates? Over."

After pinpointing the storm and learning its expected course, Mitch bit back a curse. "For God's sake man, didn't you think to warn us before now? Over."

Static was the only response.

"Come in. Hello, are you there? This is Paradise Key, come in. Over."

Nothing.

"Damn!"

"Mitch, is something wrong?" Giselle asked from the doorway.

He spun around. Dark, shiny hair tumbled about her shoulders in sexy disarray. A sleepy, inviting look glowed in her emerald eyes. Lips that were slightly swollen and red beckoned to be kissed once again. One of his shirts, carelessly draped over her very naked body, completed the vision before his eyes.

She had never looked more beautiful or more desirable. And he had never wanted her more than at that very moment.

That is, if it weren't for the damnable Brutus headed straight for them.

She took a step into the room. "Mitch?"

His eyes riveted on the tanned, long legs that stretched out from under the shirttails. Long legs that had wrapped around his waist last night, and this morning. Legs that had coaxed him further . . . deeper.

With two long strides, Giselle reached his side, then straddled his lap. Her sultry scent wafted over him, sending his pulse rate skidding wildly out of control, increasing his desire to an almost painful ache. His body hardened in immediate want.

"Looks like rain. Why don't we go back to bed?" she suggested. Her soft, husky voice zeroed in like a jolt of electricity.

His answer was lost when her lips brushed his once, then twice. He knew he ought to stop. Yes, that was what he should do. With the storm threatening their very lives, his top priority should be to reach the Coast Guard. They needed some way to get off the island before disaster struck.

But, as it was, he couldn't deny her. That would be like denying life itself.

You may not have a life left if that hurricane hits, Sullivan, a wise voice echoed in his mind.

Between kisses, he murmured, "Giselle . . . honey . . . we've got to talk—"

"Later," she whispered.

Even though his body screamed to be inside of her, he firmly took her face between his hands. "No. Now." He licked his lips and cleared his throat. "Uh

. . . the uh, reason it looks like rain is because of the hurricane.''

Giselle traced his dimples with the tip of her finger. "I figured we'd get some rain from it."

"Honey, that's not all we're gonna get. Take a look at the map."

She slid off his lap and walked to the map. Eyes wide, she whipped around. "Oh, my gosh, it's only a hundred miles or less away from us!"

"And I'm afraid it's moving due north, at fifteen miles per hour, headed straight for the Keys." Mitch got up, gazed out the window and studied the clouds. Circular feeder bands had already formed, the warm Gulf winds had picked up. The once calm, crystal-clear water had now turned dark and murky, churning and gushing to the shore as if angry, impatient. Huge drops of rain began to splatter against the window. He turned and looked back at Giselle.

"The shoot has been canceled. The crew isn't coming. Insurance won't cover them or the equipment."

Hiccup. "What—what are we going to do?" *Hiccup*.

He gave her what he hoped was a reassuring smile. "First, we're going to get you some peanut butter."

"But—" *Hiccup*.

"And then we're getting off this island."

At least he hoped they could. Looking back at the shortwave, his doubts mounted. Since he had lost contact with the call this morning, he feared the lines might already be down. He could only hope they weren't.

Giselle had once told him she didn't fear Mother Nature. If they didn't get off this island today, though, Mitch was certain Brutus would change her mind on that subject. But it would be more than just fear that would challenge her. It would be terror.

* * *

Giselle paced the kitchen, a jar of peanut butter clutched in one hand. Every now and then, she glanced out the window as if she could will the storm to pass. But, unfortunately, she didn't have that power. No matter if her last name was Grant. No, the only power she seemed to possess was the power to mess things up. And she did a bang-up job of that.

All of this was her fault. She should have told Mitch the truth from the very beginning. About the bet—and the storm. Now the shoot he had counted on to boost his career had been canceled. And if that weren't enough, Hurricane Brutus was breathing down their necks and turning the once harmless situation into one that could very well hurt them both.

Mitch strode into the room, evidently troubled and concerned.

Giselle tentatively touched his arm. "Mitch? Did you get in touch with the Coast Guard?"

For long moments, he stared at her, as if he measured his answer. Then he spoke, his voice steady, yet so soft she could barely hear him. "They're not coming, Legs."

"What do you mean, they're not coming?"

He crossed his arms over his bare chest and expelled a long sigh. "The Coast Guard has their hands full escorting cruise ships and evacuating boats at sea with full crews. They don't have the time to rescue two measly people on a *private* island."

Frantically, Giselle fumbled with the lid on the jar of Skippy. "Well, okay, so the Coast Guard can't come. Call the guy who flew us down here."

"I did."

"And?"

Several silent seconds passed. "It's too risky. The

hurricane is too close. All planes have already been flown inland. We waited too late to call."

Mitch took the jar from her useless hands, opened it and handed it back.

Hiccup. "Oh, geez." *Hiccup.* "I think we may be in trouble." *Hiccup.*

This time, the peanut butter didn't stop the hiccups.

"There's got to be something we can do . . . someone we can call." Giselle rushed to the study, her mind flying, her hands trembling. She grabbed the Rolodex and frantically flipped through it.

"Legs, stop—"

Hiccup. "It's all my fault . . . we have to call Dad. He can help us, he'll know what to do." Her voice faded and the phone numbers blurred before her eyes as the hiccups turned to tears and the tears turned to sobs.

Mitch took her in his arms and pressed his lips against her hair, murmuring words of comfort.

Nothing could comfort her. Not even Mitch or his softly spoken words. Yet, she held on to him and buried her face in the golden, downy curls of his chest. "Oh, God, what have I done?" she muttered against them. *"What have I done?"*

With two large, incredibly warm hands, Mitch lifted her face and gently wiped the tears from her cheeks with the pads of his thumbs. "You haven't done anything, honey. This is just bad timing on the part of Mother Nature, that's all."

"No, it isn't. I knew about the storm earlier—"

"You had no way of knowing it would hit here."

Giselle took a deep breath, then swallowed hard. "That's not all. I should have told you about—"

"Paradise Key, come in," came the squawking call.

"Maybe there's hope yet." Mitch smiled down at her.

Giselle rushed to the shortwave. She recognized that voice.

"Paradise Key, where the hell are you? Over."

She scooted into the chair and pressed the button on the mike. "Paradise Key, here. Over."

"Thank God, G.G. Are you okay? Over."

"So far we are, no thanks to you. Over."

"All bets are off, Giselle." Then there was a pause, followed by a commotion in the background. "Curtis, would you stop fiddling with the radio? You're going to make me lose the connection."

Curtis? Hadn't she heard that name before?

"Anita, what's going on? Over."

"It's just my pesky cousin, chomping at the bit to talk to his friend."

Her cousin?

"Never mind him. Just get your butt off that island. You win. Okay? That silly bet isn't worth your life."

Giselle felt Mitch's presence behind her. She pressed the button again, hoping to stop the flow of words, but Anita plowed ahead.

"Your dad is frantic with worry. He doesn't know you're on Paradise Key, *yet,* but I'm gonna have to tell him, G.G. And once George Grant finds out my part in this whole mess, there goes my raise out the window. Over."

Giselle closed her eyes and groaned. Well, the cat was certainly out of the bag now. Even though she had started to tell Mitch the truth a few moments ago, she had wanted to do it in her own way. Hearing it from Anita, in her friend's usual flippant manner, wouldn't help matters. But it had happened, and now there was nothing she could do about it. Besides, worry over Mitch's safety overruled any thought of keeping any more secrets from him.

The hairs on the back of her neck stood on end, and Giselle realized Mitch stood directly behind her now. She was afraid to turn around. She could practically feel the anger radiating from him, could almost see the unanswered questions hanging in the air.

Hiccup.

She spoke into the mike. "Thanks a lot, best friend. Over."

Hiccup.

The static increased, but Giselle heard a definite, "Oops." Then, in a small voice, Anita added, "Is he there? Over."

Hiccup. "Standing right behind me. Thanks for asking, *now.* Better late than never, I guess. Oh, and thanks for being more concerned about me than your raise." A fit of hiccups seized her. When she could finally catch her breath and talk, Giselle implored, "Anita, you have to tell Dad right away. So far we haven't found anyone willing to rescue us. The Coast Guard can't help us, and the charter planes have already been evacuated. We're stranded. Get Dad to use his influence somehow. Someone has got to help us! Over."

Silence. Not even static or a squeal.

"Anita! Come in. Over."

Nothing.

"Mayday. This is Paradise Key. Is anyone there? Come in. Come in. Over."

Mitch reached around her and turned the radio off. Hands placed on either side of her, he pinned her between his arms and murmured in a deadly voice in her ear, "So, *G.G.*, tell me about this bet. And who the hell are you . . . really?"

* * *

"Your name is *what*?" Mitch demanded as he loomed over her, his expression one of disbelief.

"Grant. Giselle Grant. And my father is George Grant, owner of Grant's Department Stores."

Sapphire blue eyes narrowed dangerously. "You lied to me, Legs. Why?"

Giselle shifted in the chair. "Actually, uh, it was more of a case of mistaken identity, on your part."

"I'm not believing this." He threw his hands up in the air, then splayed them on his hips. "So you're implying *I'm* the one to blame."

She cleared her throat nervously, then shook her head. "No, I didn't say that. It's kind of complicated."

Mitch straightened and crossed his arms. "Try me. Besides, we've got all day, *Ms. Grant*, that is, until nightfall when the hurricane hits. So go ahead. Tell me this fascinating story of yours."

"Well, it started with the billboard."

"The billboard? Dammit! Don't tell me—"

"Are you going to let me explain, or are you going to keep interrupting me?"

Mitch snapped his mouth shut, but his expression was as violent as the thunder that shook the house.

"My friend, rather my ex-friend, Anita, challenged me to answer your billboard ad and added an enticing bet to the dare. I've never been one to back down from a dare, so I accepted, against my better judgment."

Mitch snorted.

"I tried to get out of it, I really did. But she kept pressing me. The bet was for a substantial amount of money—money I didn't have unless I withdrew it out of my trust fund. And I couldn't do that without my father finding out about it. So I opted, rather reluctantly I might add, to answer the ad." She paused and took a deep breath. She knew she was babbling, but she had to make him understand. "Now this is the part I don't understand. You left a message on my machine, responding to my letter—"

"I never got any letters, and I never called you, Legs. Come on, now, you can do better than that."

"That's why I said I don't understand. On my answering machine it was your voice. I know it was! But when I went to your apartment for a meeting that *you* scheduled, you seemed surprised to see me. Hell, you weren't even dressed." In spite of the turmoil, a vision of a skimpy white towel flashed through her mind.

Mitch rubbed a hand over his eyes and groaned. *"Curtis,* the master of voices."

"You also mistook me for a model. After I saw your disgust over the billboard, I went along with your presumption. I knew if I told you I was there about the ad, you wouldn't give me the time of day. You made that quite plain."

"So, you decided to use me to win that blasted bet."

Giselle got up out of the chair and walked over to him. "Quite honestly, at first the bet was what pushed me into playing the part. But after the first photo shoot, it became much more than that. I liked you, Mitch. I wanted to have a chance to get to know you. And once the ball got rolling, I didn't know how to stop it. Besides that, from the way things have fallen into place, I think we were both set up."

"By who?" he scoffed.

"By our best friends, who appear to be related."

She touched his rigid arm, but he jerked back from the contact. In obvious disgust, he sighed, looked at the ceiling and muttered once again, "I'm not believing this."

"Believe me, it's the truth," Giselle implored, wanting desperately to reach out to him. "I never intended to lie to you—or hurt you."

Mitch whirled around. "But you did. Everything, every damn moment has been one big lie. Even yesterday."

His blue eyes, now chips of ice, froze Giselle's heart into a solid block of bitter cold.

Tears pooled in her eyes, and she shook her head. "No, Mitch. Not yesterday. That could never be a lie. That was lo—"

"Oh, please. You don't expect me to believe that."

"Mitch, please, listen to me."

He held up a shaking hand. "No. You don't have anything to say that I want to hear. Right now, we have to get ready for a hurricane. And after that, if we make it through alive, I don't *ever* want to see you again."

The need for pretense over, Giselle showed Mitch to a shed where the specially-made storm shutters were kept. In the same shed, they found several candles, flashlights and other emergency supplies. After many trips back and forth between the shed and the house in the driving, stinging rain, together they set about securing the house for the impending ordeal. Not speaking unless necessary. And never touching.

Time and time again, Giselle stole longing looks at Mitch. But his face was a mask, remote and terribly calm as if made of ice. The same ice that had frozen her heart in a timeless hurt. He avoided her gaze, he avoided her.

So very different from yesterday, or even this morning, she thought. Then it seemed his eyes had never left her. His touch had become a familiar warmth on her skin.

The void of her own deceit came up to swallow her, leaving her in a pit of nothingness. The cold, twisted knot that was her heart continued to beat. And Giselle was amazed. She was sure her heart had been stripped of its life by Mitch's cold rejection. She knew he had every right to be angry. But her explanation had fallen on deaf ears, the pleading looks she had given him had been ignored by eyes blinded by anger, by ears deafened by what he thought was a willing deception.

Mitch nailed the last shutter into place. Back ramrod straight, he walked into the house, without a word. Giselle blinked back the tears that threatened to join the rainwater that dripped down her cheeks. With white-knuckled hands she gripped the railing around the deck as she stood facing the Gulf, almost wishing it could swallow her up. For long moments, she watched the approaching storm, feeling its building intensity.

As Giselle watched the storm, Mitch watched her. He wanted to believe her. God, how he wanted to. But he couldn't get past the thought that she had lied from the very start. And just when he had come to feel something for her, too. More than desire. More than physical attraction. Much more than he cared to admit.

However, he had to remember, he'd vowed never to go in search of love as his sister had done so many times. It had earned her nothing but heartbreak. He had also vowed never to get involved with one of his models. But he'd done it anyway, in spite of the painful lessons he'd learned from the disastrous relationship with Celeste. She had lied and used him. Countless times.

So what was the difference this time?

Giselle wasn't his model. Not officially anyway. She had done a great job. The best he'd ever photographed. But he wasn't so sure he was objective where she was concerned. From the very moment he had laid eyes on her, she had struck some cord deep within him that had nothing to do with her abilities before the camera. No, it went much deeper than that. Straight, smack-dab to his heart.

He guessed that was why this whole revelation hurt so badly. He had tried to work out his anger, using more force than was necessary when he'd driven nails into the slots in the shutters. The pouring rain had cooled his rage for a few blessed moments. Then, slowly, white-hot anger had evolved into the icy-cold nothingness that now gripped his heart.

But even as he watched her, her once proud shoulders now slumped in defeat, her rain-soaked hair plastered against her troubled face, he tried desperately to harden his bitter resolve. He couldn't let his wants sway him.

The sky darkened with the promise of nightfall. The clouds swirled faster and faster as the wind picked up momentum and the hurricane drew closer. Normally, the northeast quadrant of a hurricane was the most threatening, especially along the outer wall of the eye. Which meant they were in for one hell of a night.

Mitch pried his attention from the churning weather and looked at Giselle again. Wind whipped her wet clothes, slapping the thin fabric against her body, but she didn't seem to notice.

A continuous roar shook the house. Closer and closer it came, louder and more intense. The noise never let up, only increased in volume like the rumble of an oncoming freight train. Mitch scanned the horizon. About a quarter of a mile out over the water whirled a massive water spout, nature's tornado of the sea. And he knew once it reached land, it would become a full-fledged twister. In a hurricane, if the tidal surge and winds didn't get you, or kill you, the numerous tornadoes it spawned would.

A part of him wished the swirling winds would sweep Giselle up like Dorothy in *The Wizard of Oz* so he would never have to see her again. But, knowing his luck, he'd end up in the same fantasy as the Scarecrow, weak-kneed and wishing he had a brain. Hell, he was already doing that.

A bigger part of him, though, still cared for her. And his concern became alarm as Giselle stood frozen in place. He waited for her to sprint inside, screaming hysterically and hiccuping all the way, begging for a spoon of Skippy. But she did neither.

Why is she just standing there? Surely she had seen the water spout.

What is wrong with the woman! The massive cloud, not to mention the thunderous sound, was hard to miss.

Mitch yanked the door open, ran to Giselle, and grabbed her by the arm. He had to shout over the ear-splitting roar. "Legs, what in the *hell* do you think you're doing?"

Dark green eyes that had once danced and beckoned, stared blankly at him, hauntingly. Incredible pain was reflected in every feature of her face. The anger and bitterness melted within him.

Mitch plunged both hands into the wet strands on either side of her head, bringing her face to within inches of his own. "Come on, Dorothy! If you don't move it, we won't be in Kansas anymore. Now, move!"

Chapter Ten

"Ouch! Watch where you're putting your foot," Mitch snapped, pushing her away from what was obviously his groin.

"Ooops, sorry," Giselle muttered as she attempted to fold one long leg back underneath her. "I feel like a pretzel." She squirmed again, trying to get comfortable.

"Be still and quit wallowing all over me."

She tried to focus her eyes on Mitch, knowing he sat barely inches away from her. Now she knew what it felt like to be a mole. She couldn't see a damn thing in the tiny half-bath, but as it is with someone who is blind, her other senses were very alive. Painfully so. The fine sensitive hairs on her arm reached out to feel the heat of his body. Her nose zeroed in on the faint smell of spicy aftershave. Her ears registered every breath he took.

But along with that, she could also sense the hostility radiating from him. He was still angry with her. Very angry. Even though she couldn't see him, she heard it in every word he muttered, felt it in the stiff way he held his body away from hers.

Automatically, her defenses came charging up like a protective shield around her heart. The shield carried with it a sword that lashed out in hurt and sliced impulsively with sarcasm. "Well, if you would turn on a flashlight, light a candle or something, I could see where to put my foot."

"I can think of several places you can put it. One

of them being your mouth. And for that, you don't need a light. In fact, I'd say that's a natural talent of yours."

"Look, you dragged me in here." She paused, then blindly searched out his arm to deliver an angry punch. "Do I have to remind you that I wanted to go to the wine cellar? Right now, in spite of Brutus, we could be having a wine-tasting party. But noooo . . . you had to be the boss, so here we are."

"There wasn't much time to think with that water spout breathing down our necks. Besides, this is the safest room in the house. Centrally located and protected, with no glass." Mitch shifted, then swore under his breath as his knee bumped against the toilet.

"You've got that right. There's no glass, but we've got a porcelain throne to keep us company. In fact, any minute now, I expect to hear the Ty-D-Bol man start to sing and tap-dance around the rim. Flip the flashlight on so in case he does appear he'll be in the spotlight." Sarcasm oozed from her every word.

"Aren't you clever?" For a moment, silence filled the room and the tension spread. His next words sliced through the silence, and her heart. "But not clever enough to get by with what you tried to pull on me."

"Mitch, I tried to explain about that—"

"Spare me any more of your weak explanations—"

"I said I was sorry."

"Sorry isn't enough, Legs."

"What do you want? My apology written in blood? Or maybe I should tear my hair out, wail, heap ashes on my head and beg for your forgiveness?" she huffed.

"That would do for starters."

She could hear a hint of a smile in his answer.

"Well, Tarzan, you'll have to wait on that one. This Jane doesn't go in for that kind of stuff."

Mitch grunted, but made no comment.

She didn't usually grovel at anyone's feet, but she wanted to reach Mitch. She had to make him understand that, while she had met him under false pretenses, her feelings were sincere and genuine. More than a bet was involved. And much more than saving herself from her father's wrath. The bet had turned on her, and her heart had been taken by surprise. She'd found love, then, at the very same time it seemed, turned right around and lost it.

"Mitch, please, why won't you forgive me?"

Only the swirling sounds of the wind that whipped at the roof answered her.

"Come on, talk to me. For the umpteenth time, I'm sorry. I know I misled you at first, but now, I'm being totally honest. I care about you. In fact, I'm falling in love with you. Why won't you believe me?"

"You just don't give up, do you?" he snapped, his voice brittle and hard.

"No, I don't. I want to know why you can't find it in your heart to forgive and—"

"Okay, Legs. You want to know why? If it'll mean I can have some peace and quiet, I'll tell you why."

Giselle still couldn't see his face, but she could feel the warmth of his breath on her cheek as if he had leaned toward her.

Each word distinct, he continued, "Remember that night on the beach when I told you I didn't date models because I'd been burned?"

"Yes, I remember."

"Well, that was an understatement. Several years ago, I met a woman who happened to be a model. I fell in love with her, and I thought she loved me. But it was all a lie. Everything. One big fat lie. She only pretended to want me so I would advance her career. Nothing more. Like a fool, I bought her a ring and asked her to marry me." He paused, and she could hear his ragged breaths. "That was when I uncovered the biggest lie of all. She was already married."

"Oh, Mitch, I'm so sorry." Giselle's heart ached for him, and guilt at her own deceit sliced through her. No wonder he couldn't forgive her. Though unintentionally, she had done almost the same thing. She had misled him. And now she was paying the price.

She lifted a hand toward him and accidentally poked him in the eye.

"Ow! What are you trying to do?" he demanded and swatted her hand away. "Gouge my eye out?"

Groping around on the floor, Giselle searched for a flashlight, a candle, anything to provide some light. She came across one solid leg, then reached over Mitch hoping to get to his stash of supplies. She reached farther and encountered what felt like a flashlight . . . well kind of . . . only . . . this was warm and familiar and . . .

The blood rushed to her face like a wave of flame, and she snatched her hand back.

This time, his voice came out in a hoarse, tortured whisper. "Legs, what *are* you doing? Trying to play post office with me or something?"

"Well, not exactly, but there's a thought."

Giselle could hear Mitch swallow, his reply lost in a strangled curse.

"What's your box number?" She grinned into the darkness.

Another curse reached her ears, and she laughed.

"Are you flirting with me, honey? Because if you are, don't bother. It won't work"

The sensual huskiness in his voice had vanished,

and Giselle's heart sank. For just a moment, the easy rapport she and Mitch had shared had struck a tiny spark of hope in her. But his last words had quickly snuffed out any spark she might have imagined.

"Please, turn on the flashlight, Mitch, or light a candle. I can't stand to sit in this darkness for one minute more."

"We need to conserve our supplies. There's no way to tell how long we may be stranded here. We might not be rescued for days."

"We have enough batteries, candles and food to last us for weeks."

"Weeks?"

Giselle let out a resigned sigh. "Don't worry, knowing my father, he'll have the entire National Guard searching for us as soon as the storm passes."

A loud crash vibrated through the bungalow, followed by the sound of splintering glass. Cool air rushed through the crack between the wooden floor and the door.

Mitch's voice came to her, steady and quiet. *"If* we survive until the storm passes."

Several hours later, still confined to the pitch black half-bath, Mitch cocked his head to one side. "Listen," he whispered.

"What? I don't hear anything," Giselle answered in a weary voice .

"Exactly. No wind, no rain—"

"Thank God! The storm is over." She jumped to her feet, then groaned as she stretched. Her bones popped and cracked from hours of being cramped in one position.

"Not quite, Legs. This is probably the eye. The worst may be yet to come." Mitch stood, cautiously opened the bathroom door and peered out, sweeping the other room with his flashlight. "Depending on how large the eye is, we should have about twenty minutes or so before the rest of Brutus gets here."

Giselle followed him out. She clung lightly to his waist as if she was afraid of the dark or perhaps of what she might find.

Broken glass crunched beneath their shoes as they walked through the kitchen. The storm shutter had been ripped away from the sliding door, and the glass had shattered, leaving puddles of water and debris all over the floor.

Mitch pointed the light downward. "Careful, the floor is wet."

"Brilliant observation, Sherlock," Giselle murmured. Water squished through her tennis shoes. "I'd say it's a tad more than just wet."

Turning, Mitch left her to explore the rest of the rooms facing the Gulf. The rubber soles of his canvas shoes squeaked with his every step as he made his way back to the kitchen. "Everything else seems to be fine. So far, this room has suffered the most damage. I'm going out to check the rest of the shutters, make sure they're secure. Since it's still dark out there, I'll need you to hold the light for me."

Five minutes later, Mitch wished he'd never asked for her help. Her nearness was driving him up the wall. Her warm breath caressed his neck as she peered over his shoulder, making sure the light was where he needed it. Her breasts brushed against his back, pinpoints of fire.

The hammer struck his thumb again. "Damn!"

"That's the third time you've done that, Mitch," she commented from behind him.

"Thank you," he said, sarcasm dripping from his words. "I'd lost count." Yeah, right.

His mind definitely wasn't on the task at hand. How could it be? For the last several hours, he'd been confined in an impossibly small room with Giselle. And every little touch, whether accidental or not, sent a shaft of intense, almost uncontrollable longing through him. The bittersweet torment threatened to melt his resolve to stay away from her. His mind shouted out her deception, but his body couldn't care less. He wanted her, and wanted her badly. Like an addictive drug or, in her case, a peanut butter fix.

He wanted to love her in the midst of the storm, joining with her as the lightning and thunder cracked about them, as the winds swept them up, faster and higher . . .

Another blow to his thumb brought him out of his erotic reverie. "Hold that light still!"

"I didn't move it an inch," she protested. "Can I help it if you're Tim-the-Tool-Man made over?"

And can I help if I mistook you for my sweet Texas lady? Mitch asked silently.

Rain began to splatter against the porch roof, coming down in giant flat drops. A few minutes later, the wind picked up and, once again, challenged all in its path to defy its strength.

Giselle swung the light out into the blackness of the storm and the night. A few feet from the railing, the beam disappeared into nothingness. Ghostly white fingers of steady rain danced in the beam.

In the flashlight's faint glow, Mitch could see her despair and worry, and for a moment, his heart softened. After all, this was her home. From what she'd told him earlier, it had been a favorite childhood retreat. Now Brutus threatened to destroy it all, the memories and the beauty, leaving just a shell of what used to be paradise.

He cupped her elbow. "Come on, Legs. Before

Brutus returns and shows us his backside, we'd better run to the shed and see if we can find another shutter or something for this doorway. Otherwise, the entire house could get flooded."

A jolt of lightning lit up the angry, churning sky. Mitch grabbed her hand and dragged her to the stairs that led down to the lawn. Heads ducked, they ran in the direction of the shed. Limbs and debris littered the once manicured lawn, hampering their progress. The inky blackness of the stormy night seemed to absorb the small beam of the flashlight, and Mitch soon found himself turned around, hopelessly lost.

He ground to a halt, and Giselle promptly plowed into him. Knocking them both to the soggy ground, she landed right on top of him.

"What are you doing?" he demanded as soon as he could catch his breath. He snatched up the flashlight and aimed it at her. Water rolled off her face and splattered into his eyes.

"Lying on top of you. What does it look like?" she sputtered, shielding her eyes from the beam of light. "Why did you stop?"

"I . . . uh, I'm not sure of my bearings," he muttered under his breath.

"You're lost?" Giselle scampered off of him and pushed to her feet. Then the giggles started. A second later, the giggles became an all-out burst of laughter. *You're lost!* Oh, this . . . ," a little snort slipped out, "this is one for the record books. And I guess you're going to do that man thing again and not ask for directions, either." Another tickled snort bubbled out.

Mitch picked himself up off the ground and pushed back the hair from his face. "I'm so glad you find this amusing. Tell me, does peanut butter cure your snorts, too?"

Her laughter ceased, but a hint of a smile still hovered on her face. "You know, I've never tried that before. But then, I haven't laughed like this in a long time."

Thunder rumbled and shook the earth beneath their feet. Lightning popped and crackled all around them. Sparks flew into the air when the jagged bolts came into contact with anything their fiery fingers could reach. The wind spun in a circular howl, whipping everything around them, snapping branches in two as if they were toothpicks.

The teasing smile disappeared from Giselle's face, and she inched closer to Mitch. "The shed is about ten yards behind you."

Quickly, they battled the wind, pried open the door and found a piece of plywood. "This will have to do, Legs. Now hold on to me with one hand and with the other, grab the wood. That wind is gonna do its damnedest to whip it out of our hands. Ready?"

Giselle bit her lip and nodded.

It took several long, frustrating minutes to make it back to the bungalow. Giselle slipped three times, and the plywood just about flew out of her hands. Brutus's backside was pretty impressive. It became an all-out war to keep their balance despite the gale-force winds.

Since the entire house was closed up and the sliding door shattered, Mitch had no alternative but to nail the wood to the inside casing. And that task proved difficult with the wind constantly pushing against it, threatening to splinter the board.

He hammered the last nail into place, and together they collapsed against the wall, breathing heavily.

"You think that's going to hold?" She eyed the wood as it bowed and creaked.

Noting her fear, Mitch couldn't bring himself to

tell her the truth. He had his own doubts. In fact, he refused to even think about what might happen if the barrier didn't hold.

And he couldn't tell her that. "Sure, it will. I've put so many nails in that sucker, it'll take a week to pry it off." Or it will tear like a piece of tissue paper at one big breath from Brutus.

A constant roar filled the air while Brutus vacuumed the oxygen from the room.

Mitch whirled around, ran into the closest bedroom, and snatched the pillows and bedspread off the bed. A second later, he was at Giselle's side, pushing her toward the tiny half-bath.

"Mitch? Is that sound what I think it is?"

Louder. Closer. The roar rattled the house. The chandelier in the formal dining room chimed as the crystal droplets cracked against one another. The air grew thinner and the atmosphere became stifling. Mitch's fear escalated.

"Move it, Dorothy, or we'll be on our way to the land of Oz. And it won't be to visit the Wizard."

Thankfully, the tornado passed over the house without ripping it apart. At least, the shelter of the bathroom remained solid.

Mitch lifted the pillow off his head and whistled. "That was a close one." He rummaged around until he found a candle and lit it. The room glowed softly as he held the flame up, surveying her. "You look like a drowned rat."

Giselle eyed him up and down, then immediately wished she hadn't. Water drops still clung to the curly blond hair on his bare chest like glistening diamonds. His wet shorts were molded to every muscle and bulge. And that all-too-familiar weakness and want spread to her every nerve ending, screaming for her to touch him, to love him once again before it was too late, before the storm ended and he walked out of her life for good.

She pushed that painful thought aside. Somehow she would make him understand. If she had to talk his ear off all night long, then she would. After all, she had a captive audience. Quite literally. But if that didn't work, on to Plan B, whatever the hell it was.

"And you look like Mr. Potato Head," she pointed out.

He grinned, then pointed to the oak, marble-topped vanity. "Are there any towels in there?"

Kneeling, she leaned over to open the cabinet door, and her bottom brushed against his thighs. She snapped to attention. "Uh, sorry."

Mitch swallowed visibly. "No problem. Let me, uh, let me see if I can move out of the way."

"Yeah? Like where? Are you going to stand on top of the toilet? May I call you Ty-D, or do you prefer Mr. Bol?"

"You're just a barrel of laughs tonight, aren't you? Look, I'll get the towels. Move back."

Mitch maneuvered around her while she got out of the way by climbing on top of the toilet seat, bending over to keep from hitting her head on the low ceiling. He opened the cabinet and felt around. "*Voilà!* Towels."

He unzipped his shorts.

"What do you think you're doing?" Giselle cried as she straightened to her full height, promptly banging her head on the slanted ceiling. "Ouch!"

"What does it look like I'm doing? I'm drying off," he answered, looking up at her. "We can't stay in these wet clothes. We'll catch pneumonia."

"But—"

"Legs, you must be delirious. Where else do you expect me to undress?"

Another violent gust of wind rattled the roof above as if reminding them their lives still hung in the balance.

"If you think I'm going out there," he pointed to the door, "just to change, think again." At her stubborn look, Mitch sighed. "Okay, okay. You go first."

Giselle stepped down from her porcelain perch and grabbed a towel out of his hand. "Fine. Turn around."

"What? Honey, if you remember correctly, I've seen every inch of your sweet body . . ." His words faded in a husky whisper.

A whisper that sent shimmering chills up her spine. A whisper that gave her hope—and an idea. *Plan B.*

She shrugged. "Suit yourself then." Never taking her eyes off Mitch, slowly she unbuttoned the blouse that still clung wetly to her skin and flung it in the sink. Her lacy bra followed, along with shorts that had to be practically peeled off her hips. All that remained were a pair of transparent lace panties.

Mitch's throat worked, his jaw tightened, but his eyes never left her. His gaze was red hot. Its dark indigo depths raked over her, worshipping her.

Taking her time, Giselle dried herself until her body glowed. She wrapped the towel around her now warm body, loosely knotting the edges at her breasts. Then she slipped off her panties, took his hand, and placed the wet lace in his upturned palm.

"Your turn," she murmured, her voice like hot satin. She stood and watched him with hungry, inviting eyes.

His fingers curled around the panties that carried her musky essence, and his body hardened in a single wild rush. He bit back a curse. Or maybe it was a groan. Mitch wasn't sure which. His only certainty was Giselle and the way she stared at him. With a look that turned his blood into rivers of fire. A look that ripped at his control.

The small thread of control vanished when she reached out a hand and touched his chest. The tip of her finger traced slow circles around his nipple. Her gentle caress made him shudder as though he'd been brushed by lightning. The very same lightning that popped and crackled in the air like the snap of a bullwhip. Blood roared in his ears, loud as the thunder that shook the heavens. And the white-hot, liquid demand rushed through him as relentless as the rain that plummeted on the roof.

His aching desire obvious, Mitch stripped off his shorts. He reached for a towel, but Giselle beat him to it, drying him with tender, achingly slow strokes, until a surging, demanding heat filled his loins, filled him.

And before he could think twice about what he was about to do, Mitch pulled Giselle down with him, spreading her legs apart to straddle his hips. As her humid, sultry heat surrounded him, wild splinters of sensation consumed him.

God! She was more exquisite than he remembered; she was lightning and rain . . . red-hot and soothingly cool.

The hot rain of her passion bathed him, drenched him, urging him deeper, harder. Yet he couldn't plunge far enough, hard enough. Wanting all of her, he rolled her beneath him, sinking into her again and again until she cried out.

As she tightened around him, he poured into her

with a pent-up wildness punctuated only by the rush of a ragged moan. Again, she had taken him to the sun, into the very center of life itself.

Sex he could have from any number of women. But this . . . sense of heart-tugging rightness was something he had only known with her. Giselle . . . His sweet Texas lady . . . The woman he couldn't let himself trust.

A repetitive, thumping sound crept into Giselle's peaceful sleep. But she pushed it aside and snuggled closer to Mitch. Her head rested against his chest, the soft cocoon of the bedspread wrapped around them. He was still sound asleep, his breathing even and deep. The rise and fall of his chest lulled her between sleep and dreams, and the sound gradually faded.

Sometime during the night, the rain had stopped, the wind had calmed. But Giselle wasn't sure when. The passion they'd shared had swept them up into a hurricane of their own, where time had no meaning.

Another, different kind of sound disturbed her dreamlike reverie, and Giselle knitted her brows. Soon it faded away again, and her lazy dreams resumed. She rubbed her nose into the soft blond hair on Mitch's chest.

The haze of raised voices reached her ears a split second before the door flung wide. Giselle shielded her eyes from the light that streamed through the opening. Two shadowed silhouettes filled the space.

"Thank goodness you're all right," came a soothing familiar voice, followed by another not-so-soothing, downright angry one.

"What in the hell is going on here?"

Giselle blinked and swallowed, pulling the bedspread up over her naked breasts.

Hiccup.

"Dad?"

Chapter Eleven

Mitch's sleepy, amused voice rumbled in her ear, "The National Guard, I presume?"

"And you thought we wouldn't be rescued for weeks," Giselle muttered over her bare shoulder.

"I asked you, Giselle," her father barked, "what the *hell* is going on here?"

"What does it look like, Dad?" She couldn't keep the comment to herself. Here she was, twenty-six years old, yet her father still treated her like a teenager. She wasn't. She was a woman. All woman. Mitch had proven that to her last night and the night before.

"I know how this must look, Mr. Grant—"

George Grant peered at him through narrowed eyes. "And who the hell are you?"

"Mitchell Sullivan, sir." He propped himself up on one elbow.

"Sullivan? The photographer? Why you dirty, good-for-nothing—" The giant of a man took a step into the cramped space.

"For heaven's sake, George." Joyce Grant reached out a hand and restrained her husband. "At least give them a chance to get dressed before you start tearing them apart."

"Thank you, Mother."

"Get dressed? Where in the hell are your clothes, young lady?"

"Dad, you're stepping on my foot," Giselle groaned, twisting out from underneath his shoe.

Hiccup.

"That's not going to work this time, Giselle."

Though he was behind her, Giselle could feel tension and anger mounting in Mitch. He stood and fortunately lifted her with him. All she would have needed was for the bedspread to fall completely off her. Then her father would really have a conniption, as if he wasn't having one already.

Hiccup.

"Mr. Grant, our clothes got soaked while we tried to save this damned bungalow of yours."

George pointed a finger in Mitch's face. "I'll deal with you later, Sullivan. How dare you take advantage of my daughter. As far as I'm concerned, you can kiss that contract good-bye."

Mitch's grip on her shoulders tightened painfully, and his face turned to granite, along with Giselle's heart. She had cost him the biggest opportunity of his career. Now she knew he would never forgive her, in spite of what they had shared last night.

One hand clutched the bedspread, with the other she grabbed her father's arm and pleaded, "No, Dad. It's not his fault. It's mine. I'm responsible for this whole mess." She lifted her chin a notch higher. "So if you're going to deal with anybody, it'll have to be with me. Not Mitch."

Hiccup.

Her father crossed his arms. "I told you, those damn hiccups don't impress me." He glared at her. "Go on."

Hiccup.

"Well, it's a long story."

"It certainly is," Mitch commented behind her. Then he looked George in the eye. "And wait till you hear it. I trust you'll find it as fascinating and *unbelievable* as I did."

"I thought I told you to shut up."

Joyce firmly took her husband by the hand. "Come on, George. You need to calm down before you have a stroke. Giselle, Mr. Sullivan, excuse us. We'll be in the office when you're ready to talk."

Giselle watched her parents walk away with a mixture of dread and amusement. They were quite a pair. Her petite mother had her father by the hand, dragging him down the hall as if he were a naughty, temperamental little boy. Yet he was anything but little. Naughty, perhaps. Temperamental, definitely. In fact, when her father was in this state there was no reasoning with him. Right now, no matter what she said he wouldn't even begin to listen. Must be a man thing. His obstinacy was similar to Mitch's.

Slowly, she turned to face Mitch. "You still don't believe me, do you?" She swallowed, forcing down the lump that had formed in her throat. Blinking rapidly to hold back the tears, she lowered her voice to a painful whisper. "Not even after last night?"

Hiccup.

"Legs, I . . ."

Tears she'd held back now squeezed past her lashes to trickle down her cheek. "It didn't mean anything to you, did it? Just a way to pass the time. Right?" She choked back a sob. "I thought that maybe . . . after last night . . . you had changed your mind, had realized I love you. But I guess I was fooling myself."

Hiccup. "Oh, blast these stupid hiccups!"

"I think they're cute," Mitch murmured as he cupped her cheek with his palm. His thumb stroked the corner of her mouth. "Giselle, I admit, I want you. Bad. Even right now." His lips curved in a little grin. "Even with those 'blasted hiccups.'"

The grin gone, his eyes flitted back and forth across her face. Then he took a deep breath and shook his head. "Last night . . . well, it shouldn't have happened. But I wanted you so damn bad, I couldn't stop myself. Hell, I didn't want to stop."

He paused and dropped his hand, leaving her cheek cold and empty. "I'm sorry, but I just can't forget the lies." Then he added, so softly the words were little more than a sigh, "I want you, but the truth is . . . I can't trust you."

"Don't . . . don't say that," she begged, her voice no more than a tortured sob.

Hiccup.

"I'm sorry."

"Yeah." She swallowed hard. "Me too."

He unwrapped himself from the bedspread, then gently tucked it around her. Grabbing a towel to cover his hips, he walked out of the bathroom . . . and out of her life.

"Mitch?"

He turned and looked at her, one eyebrow slightly lifted.

"Don't worry about your contract. Once Dad calms down and listens to what I have to say, I'm sure he'll change his mind," she told him, hoping to give him back the most important thing she had unknowingly taken from him.

"I wouldn't bet on it, Legs."

As he disappeared into his bedroom, Giselle had a feeling he was right. She also had a feeling this would be the last time she saw Mitch. Ironic. The first day they'd *officially* met, he'd been wearing a towel. Like now. It was an image that would stay with her forever, no matter what happened. She would always dream of the billboard man, dressed only in a skimpy white towel.

Her heart ached with unbearable sadness. She didn't have anyone to blame but herself. The gut feeling she'd had from the very start had been right. She shouldn't have taken the bet in the first place. Above all, she should have told Mitch the truth from the beginning.

The deception had come between them. And she'd lost. Not just the bet. She couldn't care less about that right now. No, she had lost something much more vital. She had lost her heart. Now she had nothing. No life. No love. No hope. No Mitch.

Hiccup.

No, the only thing she had left were days filled with loneliness, nights filled with haunted, empty dreams and these blasted hiccups.

"You did *what?*" George Grant exploded. He paced back and forth in the study. "Of all the stupid, irresponsible, idiotic things—"

Hiccup.

"Here, dear." Her mother handed her a spoon of peanut butter while giving her husband a black look. "Maybe this will help."

Giselle managed to swallow the peanut butter and the aching lump in her throat at the same time. "Thanks, Mom, but I don't think anything is going to help this time."

"Why do I have the feeling we're not talking about your little habit?" Joyce asked her daughter gently.

Her mother's tender concern brought fresh tears to her eyes. Giselle looked up at the ceiling, blinking furiously. "Is . . . is he gone?"

"Yes, dear. Your father's pilot took him by chopper to Miami."

Giselle bowed her head and nodded.

Her father continued his pacing. "Suppose we get on with this."

She sighed. "There isn't much else to tell. Besides, the rest of it is personal."

George Grant growled. "You were damn right to think I would have pitched a fit about letting go of five thousand dollars on such a stupid bet. I've never heard of a more ridiculous waste of money in all of my life."

Joyce cut in, "I'd say you're pitching a pretty good fit right now. Remember, George Grant, that trust fund belongs to Giselle, and it's about time you let go of the reins and let her manage it herself."

"You've got to be kidding. After what just happened? She'd be broke in a week," he scoffed. "She'd end up betting her life away. On a stupid billboard, of all things. What were you thinking?"

That was the problem, Giselle concluded. She hadn't been thinking at all. One look at Mitch and her hormones had taken over. All she'd been able to do was feel.

"Oh, for heaven's sake," her mother fumed. "You seem to be forgetting one very important thing, George." She placed her hands on her hips.

"What's that?"

"There are more important things in this world than money—"

"Name one," he countered.

"Like the fact your daughter is alive and safe after a category-five hurricane ripped this island to shreds. Have you thought about that?" She poked the large man in the chest. "*No.* You've done nothing but rant and rave at her since you've been here."

Giselle's head pivoted from one to the other, watching in wonder. She had seen her mother take charge before, but never like this.

"What kind of father are you anyway?" Joyce ended, punctuating her lecture with one last poke.

Shocked, George Grant stood still, his face beet red, his expression one of shame. "I . . . uh, I don't—I never realized . . ." His voice faded as he turned apologetic eyes on Giselle.

"It's okay, Dad. You have every right to be angry, just like Mitch does. However, I don't want to talk about this anymore, if you don't mind. No one needs to beat me over the head about what I've done," Giselle said. "I'm taking care of that on my own."

With a sad sigh, Giselle leaned her head against the cool window in the helicopter. From the air, Paradise Key looked like nothing more than a tangle of jungle. Debris and vegetation littered the once spotless sandy shoreline. Fortunately, the bungalow had only sustained minor damage. However, the rest of the island had taken a beating. And she couldn't help but wonder if her own private oasis had withstood nature's whipping.

Probably not. She sighed again. Her private paradise, the place where she had discovered the magic of love with Mitch, had most likely been ripped to shreds along with her heart.

Yearning shot through her like a jagged bolt of lightning. Hunger and love and ultimate loss churned in her, tossed her heart about savagely until the hurt threatened to consume her.

The sun shot heavenly beams through low clouds that scraped the horizon. It was hard to imagine that just a few short hours ago, the sky had been black, sinister, threatening, filled with pounding rain and swirling winds. Now, as the sun dipped lower, the world had once again returned to a peaceful and calm paradise, as if nothing had ever happened.

But it had. And it was much more than a hurricane.

Giselle's entire body ached with the tears she couldn't shed, the sobs she couldn't release, the damned hiccups that bubbled up every few seconds. All she wanted to do was crawl into some dark hole and forget, pretend she didn't feel. But the problem was she did feel—she couldn't forget. She didn't see how she ever could.

Her mother's hand covered hers, bringing her back to the present. "Are you all right, dear? Do you need some more peanut butter?"

"I'm not sure, Mom." She shook her head. "And no, this time the peanut butter isn't helping." The hiccups had refused to leave her, even though she had consumed practically half a jar of Skippy. A sure sign her nerves were stretched beyond their limits, and her hormones were in mourning, indefinitely.

"Do you love him?" Eyes that matched her own twinkled with understanding.

Giselle hesitated and looked at the back of her father's head as he sat in the co-pilot's seat in front of her.

Joyce Grant squeezed her hand. "Don't worry, he can't hear a thing sitting up there."

Looking at her mother, she asked, "How did you know when you fell in love with Dad?"

"Oh, sweetie, that's hard to explain. You just know. Your day doesn't seem complete unless you're with him. The sound of his voice sends chills down your spine, and not because he's ranting and raving, either. The sight of him makes you weak in the knees . . ." Her words faded.

"Is that how it is with you and Dad?"

Joyce gave her a tiny smile. "I know it's hard to believe, ornery as he gets sometimes, but yes, even now, after all these years, I still get butterflies when he walks into the room."

Butterflies? More like being hit by a steamroller where Mitch was concerned. Giselle leaned her head back against the headrest. "Then yes."

"Yes what, dear?"

Hiccup.

"Then yes, I love him."

"I thought as much."

"But I've lost him, Mom. Before I even had the chance to win his love, I lost him," she said, her words barely audible above the drone of the chopper.

Her mother laughed softly. "Come now, dear. Don't let that stop you. If he's lost, then that just means he needs to be found again."

Giselle shook her head. "I wish it were that easy. What if he doesn't want to be found? Besides, I can hardly blame him. I wasn't exactly truthful."

"Seems to me you had some help in that department." Joyce frowned for a moment. "I could just ring Anita's neck."

Hiccup.

"You'll have to stand in line, Mom. Right behind me."

A few minutes later the helicopter landed at the Miami Airport. They transferred to a commercial flight headed nonstop to Houston.

Giselle didn't wait with her parents as they stood in line searching for one last piece of luggage. Wanting to go home alone, she grabbed a cab instead. She desperately needed time to herself, without more dark disapproving looks and pressing questions from her father. Without the quiet concern from her mother. Although appreciated, the concern tugged on her heart and threatened to loose the dam she had carefully constructed to hold back her tears.

Giselle wanted to be alone when the dam burst, when it was overrun tear by tear, sob by sob. Exhaustion sent her emotions hurtling into overdrive. She had barely unlocked the door to her apartment when the heart-wrenching tears began.

She cried out the fear she had kept bottled up inside since the whole situation began. Cried out the terror she'd endured during the life-threatening hurricane. And she cried for the sweet love she had found with Mitch. Then, finally, the worst pain of all turned those silent tears into sobs and hiccups that shook her entire body—the pain of losing the love she had found, of losing Mitch. A man made of more than just cardboard and glue, the man who had captured her heart, her soul, her hormones; who had claimed her body like no other.

And when exhaustion overtook her, the hiccups stopped, yet the restless, haunting dreams started, giving her no reprieve, no blessed numbness, just more empty pain and a hollow functioning heart. A heart that, whether Mitch knew it or not, remained with him. A heart that would belong to no one else, only the billboard man.

The room glowed a dark crimson red. For long hours, Mitch worked relentlessly as he developed roll after roll of film. With every picture that slowly appeared in the solution, the searing knife was driven a little deeper into his heart.

Each picture spoke to him, the secret smile on Giselle's face like sunshine warming his ice-cold weary soul. He told himself not to feel, not to want. But that was impossible. Looking at her, with every picture a memory that brought the last several days into clear, blissful focus, he could almost believe he could forget the lies. Almost.

The darkroom had no clock, so Mitch had no idea what time it was. But he could tell by his throbbing head, aching body and stiff shoulders, it was well into the predawn hours. Still, he continued to work like a man possessed, like a man desperate to catch a glimpse, even if only on film, of the woman who had stolen his heart.

He unwound the last roll of film, taken at the lagoon. With trembling hands that he tried to tell himself were caused by fatigue, he swished the glossies until images began to appear. One by one, he hung the pictures up to dry. And with each one, his heart beat a little faster, a sweet heaviness settled in his groin.

The last picture formed before his eyes. The last one he'd taken that day, a second before he had dived in the water, right before he had made love to Giselle. The close-up image was only of her face. Her head was tilted back in ecstasy. Sleek hair, silky and glossy and wet, hung down her back. Water glided like sensuous fingers over her cheeks, her parted lips. Somehow, he had managed to capture the look of pure pleasure on her face. And he knew beyond a shadow of a doubt, this was the very best picture he'd ever shot.

Too bad it would go to waste. His big chance was gone. No contract, no deal. No New York, or Paris. Back to the mundane. The pet catalogs, the family portraits, the pots and pans.

He leaned against the wall and rubbed a hand over his burning eyes. From the very beginning, from the first time he had photographed Giselle, he had lectured himself, reminding his heart not to get involved. Somewhere along the way, his brain must have gotten into a major bind, and his heart had taken control.

Big mistake, Sullivan. Big-time mistake.

While her beauty and the memories of loving her threatened to melt his resolve, in the back of his mind, one fact stood out. She had lied about who she was. About everything. And he wouldn't allow himself to forget that. He couldn't afford to. He'd been down that road one very painful time. There was no way in hell he was going to get sucked up into that never-ending vortex. No way.

He gathered the stack of pictures together, flipped off the red light and walked into the living room. The first purple streaks of dawn crept through the darkness. But he hardly noticed.

He only had eyes for her smile, her bewitching long legs, her natural ease with the aspects of the island surrounding her. As he sifted through the photos, he smiled when he came across shots where he'd managed to capture her hiccups. The pictures were in rapid succession, from the first bubble of air, to the look of exasperation, to resignation, then finally to when she had dipped her finger into the peanut butter, her lips sliding . . .

Mitch knew he'd never be able to eat peanut butter again without thinking of her and how good it had tasted on her finger and lips.

He'd never be able to look at the forest at midnight and not think of her dark, green eyes.

The sound of wind whipping through the air would forever remind him of the hurricane that brought them together, and ultimately tore them apart.

The constant beat of his heart would always be a painful steady reminder that he still lived without her, without his sweet Texas lady.

Chapter Twelve

"Are we still having our pity party?" Anita's teasing voice came from behind her.

Giselle, her gaze mindlessly fixed out the window on the bustle of people and traffic below Grant's home office, barely acknowledged her friend.

"Come on, G.G. It's been three weeks."

Giselle said nothing.

"I said I was sorry. Curtis and I never dreamed it would turn out this way. Really." Anita paused for a second, then rushed on at Giselle's stony silence. "Like I've tried to tell you for the last two weeks, we were just trying to get our best friends together. We knew you and Mitch would be the perfect match."

At that, Giselle turned, her arms crossed. The all-too-familiar emptiness turned to a blazing stab of hurt at the mention of his name. "Perfect match? Well, I guess you were wrong about that. Damned wrong."

Anita shook her head. "No, we weren't wrong. Because right now, Mitch is just as miserable as you are."

For a split second, hope flared inside of her. She touched the tips of her fingers to her lips. "He is?"

"According to Curtis, he's been like a frustrated bull in a china shop."

"Speaking of Curtis." Giselle leaned over and placed both hands on her desk in the Grant style.

"Why haven't I met this cousin of yours before now? You and I have been best friends since we were kids. I've met everyone else in your family, and I find it very strange that I've never met him."

"Well, he's not . . ." Anita twisted her hands and bit the corner of her lower lip. "How should I say . . . ? Um, someone that I like to introduce to my friends."

"Why?"

"He's . . . well, Curtis is . . . uh, different. Yes, that's it. He's definitely different."

Giselle pressed on. "How so?"

"G.G., just take my word for it. While Curtis can be fun to be around at times, he is crude, rude and socially unacceptable. So I don't show him off or claim him. He has this special knack for embarrassing me."

"Oh, I see. Kind of like you do when you're with me? From the way you've described him, sounds as if he fits in just fine with you and your family." Giselle straightened and crossed her arms again.

"I'm that bad?" Anita asked.

Her wide-eyed stare softened Giselle's resolve to remain angry with her. For three weeks, she'd simmered alone, pushing away any offered apology and comfort from Anita. Apparently she had made her point. Anita looked miserable. As miserable as Giselle felt.

For the first time in weeks, her face softened into a small smile. "No, you're not that bad. And I'm sorry I've been such a grouch. You're my best friend, Anita, and I love you. I guess I just didn't expect," she cleared her throat, "love to hurt this bad."

"Pretty rough, huh?"

"That's an understatement."

Anita flopped down into the chair in front of Giselle's desk. "This is so ridiculous, G.G. You're miserable, Mitch is too. Why don't you try and patch things up?"

Blinking back the tears that sprang to her eyes, Giselle sat down. "Believe me, it wouldn't do any good. Mitch won't forgive me. For his own reasons, he can't. And I don't blame him."

"Let me talk to him then."

Giselle shot to the edge of her chair. "No! Definitely not. You've done enough, thank you very much. And besides—"

The buzz from her intercom interrupted her. "Ms. Grant, your father called and wants to see you in his office. Pronto."

"I wonder what he wants." She groaned. Ever since she'd left Paradise Key, Giselle had tried to avoid her father. To no avail. If anything, he seemed more demanding and overbearing than ever before.

The intercom buzzed again. "Ms. Grant?"

She sighed and pushed the button. "Marie, tell him I'll be right there."

A mischievous hint of a smile hovered on Anita's lips, and Giselle looked at her through narrowed eyes. "What's that grin all about?"

Anita's eyes widened innocently. "Nothing." She popped out of her chair. "Nothing at all. Call me when you get out of the lion's den."

"*Anita*—" Giselle bolted to her feet and started after her friend, but Anita had already disappeared around the corner.

A few minutes later, Giselle composed herself for another round with her father and tapped on the door to his office.

"Come in," came the command.

She took a deep breath and pushed open the door. "Dad, you wanted to see me?"

He glanced up from his desk and motioned to a chair. "Sit down."

She did so, then squirmed in the plush leather chair as several silent minutes ticked by.

Finally, her father closed the file he'd been engrossed in and folded his hands in front of him. "I want you to go down to Paradise Key and make sure the contractors have followed my instructions on the repairs."

"But, Dad—"

George Grant continued on as if he hadn't heard her protest. "And make sure the entire island has been cleaned up and restored to its previous beauty."

She jumped to her feet. "Dad, I can't go down there."

He stood and adopted his most menacing stance and stare, chest out, hands deep in his pockets, dark snapping eyes hard and cold. "Why not? I'm sure as hell not getting any productive work out of you here. You might as well make yourself useful down on the island." For a moment, his face softened. "Besides, your mother keeps insisting you need another vacation. She thinks you're looking a bit peaked." He cleared his throat. "Her words, not mine," he said gruffly.

Giselle lifted her chin stubbornly. "I'm not going."

"Excuse me?"

She swallowed. "I refuse to go unless you meet one condition."

The black look returned to her father's face as he crossed his arms. "I don't recall opening this up for debate."

"You're getting one anyway." She paused to let her unusual spurt of defiance sink in. "If you can make demands, so can I."

A strange gleam glittered in his eyes. Maybe it was fury, or perhaps admiration. Giselle couldn't tell.

"Go on."

"If you insist I go down to Paradise Key, then I insist you reinstate the contract for Sullivan Studio." There, she had said it. From somewhere deep inside, she'd found the strength to stand up to her father. Now she held her breath and waited for the top of his head to blow off.

George Grant turned and looked out the window, his hands clasped behind his back. His next words shocked Giselle into a dumbfounded state. "Done."

She licked her dry lips. "Wha-what did you say?"

He faced her, his expression curiously guarded. "I said, you win. If Sullivan still wants it, the contract is his. That is, if you hold up your end of the bargain and go to Paradise Key."

Giselle hurried around the desk and, in an unexpected show of affection, flung herself into her father's arms. "Oh, Daddy, thank you. Thank you!"

He patted her awkwardly on the back, his voice strained with unaccustomed emotion. "There, there, come on now. You act as if I've given you the world."

She pulled back and looked at him. "You have, Dad. In a way, you have."

Although she still didn't have Mitch, she'd managed to give him back the very thing he wanted most—the big chance of his career. She might have to live her life without him, but now she'd have the assurance that she'd helped put his life back on track.

George walked to his desk and opened his briefcase. "Here're your tickets. You've got about two hours to pack."

Giselle put her hands on her hips and gave him an indulgent smile. "Pretty sure of yourself, weren't you?"

"Young lady, if you don't remember anything else I've told you over the years, remember this; we are Grants, and we always get what we want."

If only that were true, Giselle thought sadly. Being a Grant couldn't give her what she wanted more than life itself—dark sapphire eyes with a dimpled smile, streaked blond hair and a muscular, tanned body. Mitch. The billboard man. The man of her restless dreams. The man she loved. The one man she would never have.

Mitch waded through the empty beer cans and discarded clothing that littered the floor, and against his better judgment answered the ceaseless pounding at the door. "Rockhead, what are you doing here? I've told you to leave me alone."

Curtis leaned against the doorjamb. "You look like hell," he commented, then glanced over the top of Mitch's head. "And so does your pad."

"Is that what you came here to say?" Mitch ran a hand over his unshaven face. "If it is, you can leave."

"Give me a break. And you need to give Giselle a break, too. It wasn't all her fault—"

Dropping his hand from the door, Mitch spun around. "I told you, I don't want to talk about her."

"Well, too bad, little buddy." Curtis slammed the door. " 'Cause whether you like it or not, you're going to hear me out."

Mitch flung himself onto the couch and looked up warily at his friend. His *former* friend.

Not only did Mitch look like hell, as Curtis had so nicely informed him, he felt like hell, too. No matter how hard he tried, he couldn't get Giselle off his mind. Of course, having her pictures tacked around the loft didn't help matters any. But he couldn't bring himself to take them down. The photos were his best work.

"You can talk all you want, Rockhead, but it won't make any difference."

The large man lumbered back and forth across the room, blocking Mitch's view of the skyline. A skyline he had memorized these last few weeks.

"You are so damned stubborn, Sullivan. It wasn't her fault, man. This whole thing started with me and my cousin, Anita. Giselle got caught up, blackmailed, whatever you want to call it, in the mess. The bottom line is when she met you, she wanted you for yourself."

"Correction," he growled. "The bottom line is she lied."

Curtis hiked up his droopy jeans and whipped off his baseball cap. "You can't compare her to Celeste—"

"The hell I can't! Celeste lied to me, so did Giselle."

"It's not the same, man. That's like comparing the good with the bad, or apples and oranges. Celeste didn't love you. She was the bad apple, rotten, wormy even," Curtis insisted, then added, "Giselle loves you and you damn well know it. And she's far from a bad apple. She's a ripe juicy orange that you're about to throw away because of your stupid pride."

"Do you have to compare everything with food?"

"Speaking of which, I'm hungry. Got anything in the fridge?" Curtis didn't wait for an answer. He loped into the kitchen and searched the refrigerator and cabinets. "Geez, what have you've been living on? Mustard and grapefruit juice?"

That was just it. Mitch hadn't been living at all. Existing maybe. But the existence had been empty, hollow. Curtis's words sank into his resisting brain and began to make some sense. A part of him realized it wasn't all Giselle's fault. At the same time, another part steered clear of accepting even the most remote possibility of forgiving her. Although he'd never admit it, the thought scared him.

But, dear God, he wanted her so badly. He missed her quick humor, her sharp intelligence, her long legs, her sultry scent. And yes, he even missed her hiccups. Damn her.

Curtis walked back into the room. "You don't have any beer left." He glanced at the crushed cans on the floor and mumbled, "And I can see why. I may run out of food at my place, but if nothing else, even *I* keep beer stocked in my fridge."

Mitch pointed to the door. "Out."

"What? What did I do this time?"

"I need to think, Rockhead—"

"Well, it's about time—"

"Out!"

Curtis shuffled to the door. "Okay, okay, I'm going. But this is becoming a nasty habit of yours, throwing me out every time I come to visit you. I may start to think you don't like me or something."

Mitch grabbed an empty beer can from the floor, aimed and threw it a split second after the door closed. "Now you're getting the picture."

The telephone began to ring, yet Mitch ignored the first several peals, dreading that it might be Giselle, afraid he would melt at the sound of her honeyed voice. At the same time, he almost wished it was her.

He snatched up the receiver. "Sullivan here."

"Finally," a somewhat familiar voice huffed. "George Grant speaking. I want you in my office as soon as possible."

Mitch attempted to slow his hammering heart.

"What for, Grant? I believe you made yourself quite clear the last time we spoke."

"Son, just get yourself down here. I've got a proposition for you."

The dial tone hummed in his ear. Anger began to simmer in him. Was he supposed to jump just because he had received a summons from the almighty George Grant? A proposition? Could he dare hope the old man had changed his mind?

Mitch strode into the bedroom to change his clothes, if he could find any clean ones. His bare existence hadn't included eating, much less laundry. He rummaged through the closet and found a somewhat rumpled shirt and jeans.

As he buttoned his shirt, he stopped and stared at his reflection in the mirror. What if he ran into Giselle while meeting with her father? What would he do? How would he react? He knew what he wanted to do—wrap her in his arms and hold her forever, forget the lies and love her. But could he?

Chances were, he wouldn't even see her. Not in an office building that size. He couldn't decide whether he wanted to see her or not. He was almost afraid to. Afraid that his brain would succumb to his heart's desire.

A half-hour later, he walked into George Grant's office.

Giselle's father stood, nodded his head and motioned to a chair. "Sullivan, take a seat. You look like hell."

"Thanks. You're the second person who's told me that."

"You should have listened to the first and opted for a shave, son."

Mitch took a few steps into the room and folded his arms. "I've been busy."

When Grant motioned to the chair again, Mitch said, "No thanks, I'd rather stand."

George shrugged. "Suit yourself. Let's get down to business then."

"You mentioned a proposition—"

"Yes." Grant cleared his throat. "I'd like to reinstate your contract."

"What brought this on?"

"Don't look a gift horse in the mouth, son. I'm offering you another chance. I've seen your work, and I like it—"

"And Giselle?" Mitch interrupted him, skeptical and wary.

"That's your business." George Grant pointed to a large box on the floor next to his desk. "These are the suits I'd like you to use. Do it your way, with any model you want. The only requirement is that you use a similar backdrop to Paradise Key."

"Wait one second. This sounds like another setup."

"Do you want the contract or not?" Grant rose to his full height, the action reminding Mitch of Giselle. "Go to whatever island you wish. You're most welcome to use my private facilities again. Just check the weather forecast before you go this time. I'm not made of money, you know."

Still suspicious, Mitch asked, "What's the catch?"

Clearly exasperated, George bellowed, "If it weren't for my daughter, I'd tell you to hit the road right now. I'm doing this for her, Sullivan. She's been moping around here for weeks, upset that I canceled your contract. This is her call."

"Look, I'm no charity case—" Mitch began.

"Dammit, I know that. No matter how upset my daughter was, if you didn't do excellent work, I wouldn't rehire you." He placed giant hands on his desk and gave Mitch an intimidating stare. "Now, do

you want the contract or not? If you do, sign here."
He flung a pen across the desk. "If not, get out of
my office." He then turned and faced the window.

The wheels in Mitch's brain rotated at an alarming,
eye-opening speed. Giselle had gone to bat for him.
Even though he had coldly rejected her explanation,
her apologies, she had still butted heads with her
obstinate father. All for him.

He scrawled his signature across the line. "Where's
Giselle? I'd like to see her."

His back still to Mitch, George Grant sighed. "She's
not in the building, Sullivan. I guess you'll have to
find her yourself."

Slamming on the brakes, Mitch stared up in disbelief at the billboard. A sense of *déjà vu* hit him. Except
this time, it was Giselle's picture that smiled down at
him. The very same photo he'd taken at the loft the
first day he'd met her. As in the infamous ad featuring
him, big bold lettering accompanied the picture.

WANTED:
THE BILLBOARD MAN
THIS SWEET TEXAS LADY
LOVES YOU!!!
INTERESTED?
MEET ME IN PARADISE

Horns blared behind him, but he hardly heard. He
just stared at her picture and reread the message
countless times, finally realizing the chances she had
risked, all for him, all for love. She'd faced her father
about his contract and had put up this billboard for
all of Houston to see, *including* her father.

Mitch's hardened heart melted, his fear subsided.

She deserved another chance. Not only that, he deserved a chance himself. A chance at the love and happiness Celeste had robbed him of so many years ago. Comparing Giselle to Celeste had been unfair. As bizarre as it seemed, Curtis had been right about that.

And now Mitch knew what he wanted to do, what he *had* to do. He had to go to Paradise.

Chapter Thirteen

Giselle stepped out of the shallow cave and into the refreshing waterfall. The cool ribbons of water slid over her skin like a fluid caress. For long moments, she stood, head tilted back and relaxed, willing away the tension that had mounted during the last two days. Tension caused by haunting memories and endless nights filled with dreams of Mitch.

Her father's contractors had done an impressive job on the bungalow. It looked almost like its old self, with a new red tile roof and storm windows all around. The thick vegetation mauled by Brutus had been thinned out, the entire island once again restored to its natural beauty. Even her private hideaway had been cleared of debris. If she hadn't been an eyewitness, Giselle could have sworn there hadn't been a hurricane at all. But there had been. In more ways than one.

Dropping down onto the ledge, she eased into the crystalline lagoon, then arched and sliced through the water like a dolphin. Emerging, she rolled onto her back and floated.

The drone of an airplane sounded overhead. Since the storm, it seemed as if aircraft of some sort constantly dotted the sky, flying in supplies and construction crews to rebuild the chain of islands that made up the Florida Keys. The entire coastline had taken a beating, and it would take months to clean up the mess left by Brutus.

Paradise Key's contractors and landscapers had gathered their equipment and left that morning. Now she had the island to herself. She was totally alone, with nothing to do but relax, as her mother had repeatedly encouraged her to do. But that was impossible. Idleness made her think, feel, want. And that was something she couldn't afford to do. The cost was too high, the hurt too heavy.

She'd thought keeping busy at the office would keep her mind off Mitch. For the last few weeks, she'd made a pretense of working, but that was all it had been. Just pretense. And her father had seen right through it. She guessed that was why he'd sent her here. She'd been nothing but dead weight on the job. A big no-no in the Grant Book of Rules. But no matter how hard she'd tried, she just hadn't been able to concentrate. Her heart kept getting in the way. And being on the island hadn't changed a thing.

Mitch was always with her, his image startlingly clear in her mind. Dark sapphire eyes, dimples to die for and a hard, tanned body barely covered in a skimpy white towel.

Floating to the rocky edge of the lagoon, Giselle kicked off in the opposite direction, absently paddling her feet. Streamers of sunlight glittered off the surface of the natural pool, warming her skin, reminding her of another touch. In frustration, she splashed some water over her in a futile effort to cool her flushed skin and her heated thoughts.

The last two days her father had kept in constant contact as if he doubted her ability to handle his assigned task on her own. And through those short conversations, Giselle had learned that Sullivan Studio's contract had been officially restored. She smiled. Her father had kept his word. As for herself, she had managed to undo at least part of the damage caused by her deception. Maybe one day Mitch would find a way to forgive her. Maybe.

Yeah, right. Who was she kidding?

A chill shimmied over her, and Giselle had the distinct feeling she was being watched. She groped for the sandy bottom and spun around. Maybe she wasn't quite as alone as she had thought. What if one of the construction workers had stayed behind? Perhaps he had other things on his mind than lumber and nails.

A twig snapped and the bushes shook next to the clearing by the only exit. Giselle swallowed and backed up until she reached the ledge next to the waterfall, ready to pull herself out and make a dash beneath the cascade of water when a figure emerged.

"Mitch?"

Hiccup.

"Who did you expect? George of the Jungle? Honey, you have one vivid imagination." He gave her a wondrous dimpled grin, and relief spread through her.

Giselle wiped at the water that had gotten into her eyes. Surely she was seeing things. She blinked, then blinked again. Mitch still stood there. He wasn't a dream either. And he was actually *smiling* at her.

Although he hadn't moved any closer, she felt surrounded by him until she shivered with a want that showered through her like a warm summer rain. The cool water that lapped at her became a heated caress and it was all she could do to keep from launching herself into his arms.

Hiccup.

"What . . . what are you doing here?" From the moment he'd appeared, she hadn't been able to tear her gaze from his face, his eyes, his dimpled smile. However, now she noticed the camera bags slung over his shoulder, the giant mesh bag he held in one hand.

A frown replaced the grin. "I thought you wanted me, or at least, that's what the billboard said."

"Billboard? What billboard?" Giselle pushed away from the waterfall and swam toward the center of the lagoon until her feet touched the bottom. *Hiccup.* "I don't know anything about a billboard, but I do want you." She paused and took a deep breath, then walked slowly until she could see into the depths of his eyes. "I never stopped."

There. She had laid her heart on the line, a willing sacrifice for love. Deep inside she feared another cold rejection, but she didn't care. She couldn't feel any colder than she already did. Without Mitch. Besides that, love couldn't be won without taking chances.

Mitch ran a stiff hand through his hair. "Don't tell me . . . you mean you didn't . . . ?"

She shook her head.

"But who?" A burning curse slipped from his tight lips. "Curtis."

At the same time, Giselle groaned, "Anita."

He studied her for achingly long seconds, and her heart all but stopped in her chest. Her hiccups bubbled up in rapid succession. To her surprise, Mitch threw back his head and laughed. "I guess we've been duped again."

Her pulse pounding, she took a few steps toward him and smiled back. "Looks that way, but if that's what brought you back to me, then I'm glad."

He eased the camera bags and the other one to the ground and folded his arms, his expression watchful, his blue eyes hot and hungry. "Me too. But more than a damned billboard made me come to you. I want you, Legs. Dammit, I tried not to. God, how I tried. I came up with every excuse for wiping you out of my life, trying to pretend nothing happened between us. But I was only fooling myself. I was never more myself than when I was with you."

Caressed as much by his words as she would have been if he'd touched her, she trembled. And he could have touched her, he was just an arm's length away. "I . . . was afraid to hope—" *Hiccup.*

"It's not going to be all play though, Legs. We've got work to do, thanks to you." He knelt down and tapped her on the nose.

Hiccup. "We?"

"Your father offered me another contract."

"I know," Giselle said softly, unknowingly arching and lifting her mouth to him in a silent invitation. A playful caress on her nose just wasn't enough. Not nearly enough.

Wanting him to make the first move, she squelched the desire to pull him into the water and kiss him, hold him, give herself to him. "I couldn't have lived with myself if you hadn't gotten another chance. After all, I was the reason you lost the big one in the first place."

"You stood up to the infamous George Grant, Legs. Knowing him, it had to be difficult. But you did it. And I know you did it for me." Mitch got to his feet and gestured to the large bag. "Right now, we'd better get busy. We're already three weeks behind schedule. Here are the suits."

Giselle knitted her brows. "Suits?"

"Stipulations of the contract. I get to choose the model." Mitch grinned. "And I choose you."

Her mouth dropped open, another squeaking hiccup escaped and Mitch's grin widened. "But . . . but I can't. I mean, I'm not—"

"A typical model," he finished for her. "You are now, Legs. So get your sweet little bottom out of that water and into these suits. Since you're already *wet*, we'll do those shots today. Right now, in fact. Under the waterfall . . ." His words faded as he watched her climb out of the lagoon. And he swallowed hard. Wet shots, indeed. The immediate rush of hot liquid want spread through him and gathered into a hard knot in the lower half of his body.

Giselle wore the same white bikini she'd worn that day three long weeks ago when he had made love to her in this very place, in this very paradise. As before, her nipples peaked like perfect crowns beneath the nylon, their blushing areolae inviting circles to his hungry mouth. The rest of the suit left little to the imagination. Beads of water rolled off her full breasts, trickled down her flat stomach, to slowly *drip-drop* like hot honey down her long, luscious legs. Legs that had haunted his dreams night after night. Legs he had so desperately missed. Legs he wanted wrapped around him.

Mitch bent down and searched through one camera bag. Retrieving the jar, he twisted the lid off and swirled a finger in its contents. Holding out the finger topped with peanut butter, he softly said, "Come here, Legs. Although I must admit I've missed them, it's time to get rid of those hiccups."

A light pink flush stole into her cheeks, and at that moment, Mitch thought she had never looked more beautiful, or vulnerable.

"How," she swallowed, then took a hesitant step

closer to him, "how did you know to bring the peanut butter?"

"Because I know you, honey." Then he added in a whisper, "Inside and out."

Another step closer and Giselle took his offered finger into her mouth, sucking gently, twirling her tongue over the tip. Ever so slowly, she released his finger, and while her lips still lingered, warm and wet, against his skin, she asked, "Is that all you missed, Mitch?"

Her forest green eyes watched him closely, knowingly; and her bottom teeth lightly scraped over the pad of his finger. The fire that had been simmering for weeks now exploded into a blazing inferno. An inferno that only Giselle could control.

When he could find his voice, Mitch murmured, "You know better than that, Legs. I missed your smile, your sense of humor, your intelligence. I missed everything. The way you look into my eyes, the way you make love to the camera, the way you make love to me . . ."

His hands skimmed over her cheeks and down her neck to her arms. He pulled her closer until her body brushed against his. Electric shock waves vibrated through him. His voice deepened as his desire escalated. *"Everything.* Your gorgeous long legs, your body."

For a moment, she smiled, but a slight frown soon took its place, and she pulled back. "I need more than that."

"I know." He paused, and took a deep breath, weighing the risks, ignoring the past. "Not only did I miss you, honey, but over these past few weeks, I found that I need you, too."

"More," she whispered, her finger tracing his cheek.

"I want you . . ."

"You already said that."

"I trust you, forgive you."

"And?" She looked up at him, her green eyes bright and wide and expectant.

Mitch bent his head, his lips just a breath away from hers. "And most of all, I love you, my sweet Texas lady."

She flung her arms around his neck, and he caught her responding cry with his mouth. Crystal tears cascaded down her cheeks, wetting his face until Mitch wasn't sure whether the moistness was Giselle's or his own.

Reluctantly he dragged his lips away from hers, only to scatter tiny kisses over her cheeks, her brows, her wet lashes. Then he gazed down into her eyes and cupped her face, his thumbs gently wiping away her tears. "Sweet Texas lady, will you be my sweet Texas bride?"

Hiccup.

"Oh, yes, billboard man. Definitely yes!" A wide smile transformed her face. "But does this mean I still have to be your model?"

"You've got that right, Legs. Starting now, ending never. A lifetime contract, a binding proposal. I promise to capture you with the camera, the way you've captured my heart with your love."

Through lowered lids, she sent him a blazing, hungry look. "A lifetime contract, huh? Where do I sign?"

He gave her a wolfish smile. "Actually, you have to sign in several places." He took her hand and lowered it. "Starting here."

"Oh, Mitch—" *Hiccup.*

"What a nice signature you have," he muttered between clenched teeth as her hand lovingly stroked his aching hardness.

"Hmmm . . . so where else do I have to sign?" she breathed into his parted lips. Her fingers continued to work their magic.

Desire gripped him until he found himself shaking. "Anywhere you want, honey. Just tell me one thing. I want to hear it."

Hiccup.

"I love you, Mitch. And I'll always be your sweet Texas lady."

ABOUT THE AUTHOR

Donna Delaney lives in her very own paradise in Pasadena, Texas, with her tall, dark, and handsome Texan, and her "Don't-Bother-Me-I'm-Sleeping" Garfield impersonator, Sammy. She sings professionally, and enjoys love, laughter, and most of all ... LIVING!